Final Cycle

Elaine L. Orr

Copyright © 2023 Elaine L. Orr
Initial copyright in 2018.
All rights reserved.
ISBN-13: 9781088203149
Library of Congress Preassigned Number:
2019902135

FINAL CYCLE

ELAINE L. ORR

BOOK 2 OF THE LOGLAND
MYSTERY SERIES

Final Cycle is a work of fiction. All characters are
products of the author's imagination.
All rights Reserved.

www.elaineorr.com
www.elaineorr.blogspot.com
ISBN 13: 978-1-0882-0314-9
Library of Congress Preassigned Number:
2019902135

Elaine L. Orr

Dedication

*To my husband and family, always.
And to those fighting private internal battles. You might be surprised to know there are those willing to help, if only you would ask.*

Acknowledgements

Special thanks to the Decatur Critique Group (Angela, Dave, Debbie, Marilyn, and both Sues), and to Karen Musser Nortman, a terrific beta reviewer. Thanks also to Ronny, for the pie expertise.

While the Logland series is not based on any one central Illinois town, in my head I have pictures of places like Jacksonville and Virden – both of which have good independent bookstores.

CHAPTER ONE

LOUELLA BELLE SIMPSON did not win any popularity contests during her years as the combined home-ec and health teacher at Logland High. The trend continued after she retired.

Dislike for her centered mostly on her constant attempts to educate (her word) parents on how junk food would lead to sick and overweight children. Everyone in the Bully Pulpit Diner, her favorite soapbox since retirement, agreed with her in principle. She had a survey to prove it. Most patrons agreed to take it simply to shut her up.

Eventually, diner operators Nick Hume and Marti Kerkoff told her she could only talk to other patrons if they stopped at her booth or called her over to theirs. Stopping at her booth was not considered voluntary when she told dry cleaner owner Squeaky Miller that his shoe was untied and he should fix it before he tripped.

On Monday, one week before Christmas, Nick, usually friendly to everyone, stood at her booth to take her lunch order. "Ms. Simpson, I'm here to find out if you want the chili or taco salad, not get told off for eating a donut."

The feather in Louella Belle's brown felt hat shook as she asked, "Do you know how many grams of carbohydrates are in one jelly donut?" She tapped the menu. "Not that you can tell by looking at this. Where's the nutrition information, young man?"

"If you don't want the chili or taco salad, how about the grilled ham and cheese? The ham's straight from the oven."

"The sodium..." Louella Belle began.

Nick turned toward the lunch counter and the kitchen behind it. "I need to bring ice water to the large booth in the back. I'll stop by your table again after I do that."

She muttered into her menu. "He'll need a bigger coffin if he keeps eating that junk."

Cookie shop owner Doris Minx spoke from her spot in the next booth. "Louella Belle, he's not dying soon. Nick's barely twenty-one. I have some new sugar-free cookies. If you stop by I'll give you a free sample."

Across from Doris, Mayor Sharon Humphrey rolled her eyes at the baker.

Louella Belle turned her head far enough around to look at both of them. "Those artificial sweeteners just make you want real sugar."

Ever the diplomat, Mayor Humphrey said, "Lots of choices at Doris' cookie place."

"And all bad for you," grumbled Louella Belle.

Marti's voice cut into the conversation. "Can I take your order before I pick up the diner's laundry across the street?"

Marti and Nick used red-and-white-checkered tablecloths for the large table at the far end of the diner's long L portion and on booths at each side of the short part of the L, the cigar component, as Nick called it.

Louella Belle raised a sagging chin to meet Marti's gaze. "You two would spend a lot less money managing this place if you'd go back to plain table tops instead of wasting detergent doing laundry."

Marti tapped her foot, her trademark indication of impatience. "Maybe you'd like to run a couple of errands and then decide what you want to order."

Louella Belle shut the thin plastic menu sharply, then slammed it on the table. The harsh slap did not seem to have expressed her outrage sufficiently. She slid to the edge of her booth. "Move over girl. I know when I'm not wanted."

None of the regular diners would have found this believable.

Marti stepped back so she could climb out of the booth. "Your patronage is always welcome, Louella Belle, just not the commentary."

Final Cycle

Louella Belle, all five feet two inches of her, reached into the booth for her brown cloth coat with its faux-velvet collar. "I'd rather be outside in the cold than in here." She shrugged her arms into the coat, shooting Marti a dagger-eyes look as she did so.

"Watch out for slippery spots. We cleared the diner's sidewalk real well, but Gene hasn't been to the tattoo parlor yet, so his walk is still covered in snow."

"Humph." She stomped toward the door, stopping long enough to tell a young couple that they shouldn't give their kids diner food. "You should buy some of my organic vegetables next summer."

A boy about three years old opened his mouth wide to show her the mix of chocolate milkshake and peas he had crammed under his tongue.

Louella walked out the door and managed to pull it to a sound slam behind her.

No one spoke for several seconds, until Mayor Humphrey said, "She'll come back in a few minutes."

Nick walked past Marti with a tray bearing four glasses of ice water. "Maybe we need a moat."

"It wouldn't be so bad if she didn't scare off other customers." Marti glanced at the parents and their two toddlers. "I'm sorry about that."

The man wiped dribbles of chocolate milkshake off of the three-year old's chin. "Be glad you didn't have her for health class."

The glass door opened and aging newspaper editor Jerry Pew came into the diner, stomping his feet on the black mat in front of the door. "Afternoon Marti, Mayor." He glanced around. "Nice Christmas tree in the window, Marti."

She gestured toward an empty booth near the door. "Thanks, Jerry."

Doris turned so he could see her face, and waved lightly.

Jerry grinned. "Ah, my favorite baker. Hello Doris." He turned to Marti. "How 'bout some of that tomato soup for starters? This old guy is chilled to the bone."

"Sure thing, Jerry." Marti made for the kitchen, Nick behind her. When she walked ahead of him, they looked like a costume-party horse, short in front with a tall rump and tail rising at the back end.

Monday afternoon had turned to dusk before Marti remembered the load of tablecloths and kitchen towels in the laundromat across the street. She and Nick had been pleased when Squeaky took over a vacant store next to the dry cleaners and added five washers and four huge dryers. But, they didn't like to leave dry clothes in the tumbling drum. Too many wrinkles and a temptation for any light-fingered laundry doer.

She took off her apron and turned to Nick, where he sat at the counter with his afternoon ham sandwich. "I'll probably be over there for ten minutes. I want to fluff up the tablecloths so they aren't so wrinkled." She pushed a button on the cash register to open the drawer and remove a quarter.

"No problem. It's our quiet five minutes before the six-o'clock rush." He downed a gulp of the sandwich in one bite.

Marti grabbed her ski jacket from the hooks across from the entry door. She waved at Gene as she crossed the street toward the laundromat. After a day of cold, any unshoveled snow had ice underneath. In front of Man Up Tattoos, even owner Gene, with his broad shoulders, seemed to have a hard time chipping at the layer below the white stuff.

The laundromat's warmth felt good to Marti. She strode to the commercial dryer where she had placed the diner's tablecloths several hours ago and inserted the quarter.

The thumping sound made her wonder whether the lint catcher had fallen into the spinning drum. She peered into the round window in the dryer door in time to see the surprised-looking face of Louella Belle Simpson cycle by.

CHAPTER TWO

POLICE CHIEF ELIZABETH FRIEDMAN studied the wet countenance of the late Louella Belle Simpson. Before Elizabeth arrived, two officers had wrestled her body from the dryer in response to Marti's hysterical call.

The woman now lay on her back across the laundromat's wooden table that usually held folded clothes. Gray hair fell in clumps on her forehead and cheeks, and unseeing eyes appeared to focus on the ceiling. In death, her skin acceded to gravity and eased the wrinkles in her eighty-year old face.

Elizabeth's quick examination of the dryer door had convinced her it would be difficult to close it tightly from the inside. Besides, the device had to be started from the outside. Louella Belle definitely hadn't begun any spin on her own.

Since Louella Belle's hair and the upper part of her coat were still wet, Elizabeth thought she probably hadn't been in the dryer too long. Someone else would have found her.

She hoped Louella Belle was dead, or at least unconscious, when someone stuffed her in the dryer. Determining that would be up to Dr. Isaac Hutton, a.k.a. Skelly, the county medical examiner and coroner.

Elizabeth watched him gently prod the back of the skull, probably looking for indentations. She saw no blood on the floor, though her officers would have to determine if any had been recently cleaned.

Still probing, Skelly glanced up at Elizabeth. "I probably won't know anything until I finish her autopsy. No ligature marks on her neck, though her dousing and spinning could disguise all kinds of things."

She nodded, noting the lock of black hair that fell on his forehead when he bent over Louella Belle again. Skelly came to Logland about four years ago, Elizabeth not long before. They'd become friends, but Elizabeth wouldn't let herself think of him as more than that. Not someone she had to work with. She'd fallen into that trap in Chicago, and she wouldn't again.

"Can you determine much while you're here?" Elizabeth asked.

"Her time in the dryer, to say nothing of the water, complicates everything. It'll be hard to tell if what looks like a broken arm took place in the dryer or before she went in there."

Elizabeth frowned. "Even without her head and shoulders being wet, it'll be almost impossible to isolate fibers or hair to a perp. I bet at least two dozen people wash clothes in here every day."

Skelly finally stopped probing and called to the two police officers stationed near the laundromat front door. "How about some lifting help, guys?" To Elizabeth he added, "I'll let you know what I find out as soon as I can."

He would call with preliminary thoughts later that evening and probably finish his work sometime the next day. She hoped so. With Christmas so close, she wanted to figure out what happened to Louella Belle before she had to cancel vacation plans for the small Logland, Illinois police force. And to catch a murderer, of course.

Officers Tony Calderone and Christopher Mahan, whom she'd called back to duty after their shift ended, walked to the folding table from the door, where they'd been standing sentry. Now that orange cones and police tape kept curious eyes a good distance away, they could leave their posts to help move Louella Belle again.

As Calderone stared at Louella Belle's contorted expression, he spoke to Skelly. "I saw Jerry Pew outside. You want me to get the gurney from your van for you, so you don't have to blow off everyone's favorite newspaper editor?"

Final Cycle

"That'd be great. There's a black body bag sitting on the gurney," Skelly said. "When I walk out I'll tell Jerry to call Elizabeth later."

"Oh, joy," she said.

Elizabeth moved past the now-silent washers and dryers to the locked entrance and looked out one of the two plate glass windows. To her right was Squeaky's dry cleaning business, with Gene's Man Up Tattoo Parlor next on this side of the street.

Next to the tattoo place was an empty building whose windows the Chamber of Commerce decorated for each change of season. Then Combine Street emptied into the town square.

Almost directly across the street was the Bully Pulpit Diner, ensconced between an independent insurance agency on one side and a tiny shop that sold fabric, yarn, and crafting supplies. Farther down the street, away from the town square, were Dollar General, Doris' Cookie Shoppe, Ringlet's Beauty Salon, Alice's bookstore, and the pizza place.

Buildings along Combine Avenue weren't attached like row houses in larger cities, but they abutted one another, with occasional access to the street between buildings. Usually the space was a vacant lot, the result of a fire or maybe a demolition if the city condemned a building. When an ancient five-and-dime store came down last year, Elizabeth joined the crowd that gaped at a World War II-era painting of Rosie the Riveter on the building next door.

No matter where she looked, Elizabeth saw nothing out of the ordinary -- other than the small crowd that had gathered across the street. A killer could stand nearby, but wouldn't have a sign that said "arrest me."

Only a Logland winter streetscape met her eyes. The light snow had turned slushier earlier, but was back to a mix of frozen snow and ice. The old-fashioned street lamps each held a huge artificial wreath of holly leaves and huge red berries, complete with a red bow and a plastic candle the size of Elizabeth's cat.

As Calderone and Mahan pushed the gurney with Louella Belle's body bag on it toward the alley exit, someone crossed the street, ignoring the traffic cones and police tape. Elizabeth squinted. City Clerk Donald Dingle walked directly to the laundromat front door and pressed his nose to the glass. "Let me in."

Dingle had been city clerk for forty-two years. Full-time nuisance was the least offensive term Elizabeth used for him.

From behind Elizabeth, Skelly muttered, "He's all yours." He took off his gloves and placed them in a plastic bag in his black medical satchel.

She nodded at Dingle through the door. "Crime scene, sir. How about heading to my office? I'll be down there in a few minutes."

Dingle scowled. "Is it really Louella Belle?"

"I'm sorry, yes. Corporal Grayson will be here soon with some paper to cover the windows. Sorry you had to hear from someone besides me."

"I need to see her," Dingle said.

Elizabeth turned slightly, and met Skelly's surprised expression. It probably matched hers.

Skelly walked to the door and stood next to Elizabeth. "I'll have her at the hospital in about half-an-hour. Why don't you come by there in an hour or so?"

Dingle seemed to want to say something else, but he shut his mouth, turned abruptly, and walked away.

"You'd let him see her?" Elizabeth asked.

Skelly shook his head. "After I check a couple things, I'll comb her hair and take a photo to show him, something like that. Were they friends?"

Elizabeth shrugged. "I would have said adversaries. She attended a lot of city council meetings to…offer ideas."

Skelly turned toward the back exit. "Last suggestion she gave me was to force the hospital to take out all the snack machines in the doctors' lounge."

Officer Grayson came in as Skelly followed Louella Belle out the alley door. Elizabeth helped the five-six Grayson tape blank newsprint paper to the windows. Jerry Pew was smart. He'd provided the paper, now she owed him a favor.

"Where's Squeaky, Chief?"

"He was pretty shook up. Asked me if I minded if he grabbed a pint at the bar in the Weed 'n Feed. I told him one only. You know how he is."

Grayson grunted as he stuffed a roll of masking tape into the pocket of his dark blue, waterproof, bomber-style jacket. "You hangin' out here for a while?"

Elizabeth shook her head. "Calderone'll be back in a few minutes. He's going to stop by the station to get the crime kit. I want you guys to get prints from all over the dryer, not just the handle."

She headed to a different dryer and placed a palm flat against the front portion, which the dryer door latched into. "Somebody may have had to lean against the door to shove her in."

"A couple somebodies, probably." Grayson scanned the approximately sixty-by-fifty foot room, cluttered with equipment, tables for folding clothes, and laundry baskets on wheels. "We'll think of more stuff to check."

Elizabeth smiled inwardly. Grayson was a decent cop, but he'd never stretched his mental capacities. "Calderone took that three-day course up in Springfield. The one in evidence gathering."

"Sure." He grinned momentarily. "He knows how to boss us."

Elizabeth raised her eyebrows.

"But he don't of course. He just knows what to do."

The alley door opened and Calderone and Mahan returned, Mahan carrying the bulky crime scene evidence bag. He put it on a table a couple dryer lengths down from Louella Belle's former place of repose.

"Thanks, guys," Elizabeth said. "I don't know how much meaningful evidence will be in a place with lots of people in and out."

"Plus all of us moving around," Mahan said. He pulled out thin paper shoe covers. "Should we bother with these?"

She nodded. "Yep. I talked to Grayson here about prints on the dryer. Could be some around the big laundry tub." Elizabeth nodded to the large sink in the back corner. "My guess is that's where someone dunked the poor woman."

Mahan grimaced. "Think they held her under until she drowned?"

Elizabeth shrugged. "Lots of options, I guess. They could have killed her with a blow to the head or chest, and want us to think they drowned her. Go ahead and collect hair samples from the dryer and tub area. Calderone, you're lead. Pursue any of those ideas you studied up in Springfield."

Elizabeth didn't want to appear cavalier, but she didn't expect to learn much. "You brought Luminal, right?"

Calderone nodded. "Best blood residue detector in town." He glanced around the room. "She wasn't obese, but nobody would call Louella Belle a pixie. They had to get her from the laundry tub to the dryer."

"Another good point." She glanced at the floor. "I don't see any scuff marks."

"Could've used one of the laundry carts," Mahan said.

"True," Elizabeth said. "Grayson, work with these guys as long as needed, but get back on patrol as soon as you can. I want you to swing by Louella Belle's place. If it looks as if someone's in there, call in."

"She live alone, you think?" Grayson asked.

Mahan nodded. "No local family, as far as I know. Small bungalow about six blocks from the high school. Kids didn't trick or treat there. She gave granola bars."

"You want us to search it tonight?" Calderone asked.

"You can work up a warrant for tomorrow, if the state's attorney's county person thinks we need one. She's not going to be accused of anything, and I'd bet her murder was unplanned. I doubt anything in her house will tell us much, but we should check."

"Where you headed?" Mahan asked.

"To collect Squeaky, then talk to Marti. I told her to go home and lie down and I'd visit with her there."

Calderone shook his head. "When I drove by the diner a minute ago, I looked through the window. She was at the cash register."

"Nuts." Elizabeth wanted her at home partially because Marti's tears and shaking needed a rest, but also so she wouldn't talk to a lot of people before Elizabeth got to interview her. "Guess I'll grab her first."

CHAPTER THREE

ELIZABETH LEFT BY THE ALLEY door to avoid the last few gawkers across from the laundromat. Each of the rear doors to the businesses she passed had back door lights, but the alley had no street lamps. It didn't look as if any business had added external security cameras recently, so no help from any video.

She walked briskly. Even in boots, her feet quickly absorbed the cold and she stomped them a couple of times.

Elizabeth glanced at the tall plastic trash bins and a few recycling tubs. Squeaky's tub held several bunches of carefully tied wire hangers. A half-rusted bicycle leaned against the brick wall of Gene's Man Up Tattoos.

Mid-block, a narrow strip led back to Combine Street. Elizabeth crossed to the Bully Pulpit Diner. Decades earlier, a long-gone owner had remodeled the interior so it had red booths, tile floors, and the traditional lunch counter and stools.

She entered the Bully Pulpit, sidestepped an artificial Christmas tree a few feet inside the diner, and was pleased to see Squeaky a couple of booths back, nursing a cup of black coffee. No other patrons. Either Christmas shopping or concern about a murder nearby had kept folks away.

Squeaky's dour expression said he would rather be almost anywhere else, too. He jerked a thumb toward the kitchen.

Elizabeth walked behind the lunch counter and pushed open the swinging doors that sat directly behind the cash register's spot on the counter. She had not had any reason to be in the diner's kitchen for months. Steel appliances still lined the walls, but it had less of a hospital kitchen look. It now sported bright yellow wall paint, plus base cabinets that had gone from a sort of dirty tan to mossy green.

Only a few thousand people lived in Logland, so it had only a couple of unexpected deaths each decade, usually from something like a fall from the bleachers during homecoming at Sweathog College, or maybe a hit-and-run. To have two murders in a year seemed impossible, and that Marti and Nick had been associated with the two deceased was…odd.

Not that Elizabeth would initially suspect either of them in Louella Belle's murder. Considering that the diner was a hub of activity for most local business people and a number of other townspeople, their connection was more likely than that of, say, a dairy farmer just outside of town.

She nodded to Marti and Nick. He wore a Santa hat at a jaunty angle, and Marti's apron featured a winter scene with a wide-eyed deer. They each sat on a tall stool facing the steel prep table in the center of the large room. Marti dabbed at tear-streaked cheeks, her green eyes bloodshot and dark brown hair now limp, hanging in clusters on her shoulders.

Elizabeth walked to them and leaned on the table. "How're you doing, Marti?"

She sniffed loudly. "I know you told me to go home to rest, but I didn't want to be by myself."

"And I wanted to keep an eye on her," Nick added.

Elizabeth stifled a smile as Marti straightened her back. She was usually the take-charge partner, and probably didn't think she needed anyone to watch out for her – most of the time, anyway.

Elizabeth pulled up a third stool and took a notebook from her pocket. "That makes sense. I hope you've been at least taking it kind of easy. You had a big shock."

Marti shrugged. "It's not like we had a lot of customers."

"We talked for a minute when you were at the laundromat, but I'd like to go over things in more detail."

Marti pulled a folded piece of paper from her apron pocket. "I tried to think of things." She shivered. "I remember the kinds of questions you asked when Ben died."

Nick's look at Elizabeth struck her as sort of accusatory.

"That's good, Marti. Why don't you talk about what happened, and I'll ask questions when you're done."

Marti took a breath. "Okay, so I told you I went over there for the tablecloths I had put in the dryer maybe three hours earlier."

"And kitchen towels," Nick added.

She nodded. "I was going to head over earlier, but when Louella Belle had her hissy fit…"

"She was here?" Elizabeth asked.

Marti glanced at her list. "She left about two?" She looked at Nick, who nodded. "She was here for a late lunch."

"Left mad," Nick said. "We wanted her to order and she just wanted to complain about the menu, stuff like that. We didn't ask her to leave, just to order."

"Who else was here when she was?" Elizabeth asked.

"Us, of course," Nick said. "The mayor and Doris sat kinda behind Louella Belle. Doris told her she could stop by the bakery for a free sugar-free cookie."

Elizabeth jotted notes. "Good. I'll see if she went there."

"Anyway," Marti continued, "I didn't see her again until, well, you know."

Elizabeth nodded, not wanting to break Marti's flow.

"So when I got over there, I could see one of the checkered cloths in the dryer window. I put a quarter in just to fluff them up a bit, and I pushed start. And that's…that's when I heard the noise."

Elizabeth nodded again. "I think you said kind of thumping."

"Yes. For a second I thought the lint trap fell into the drum, then I figured that was odd, because it's kind of at the bottom of the drum, in front. You'd have to put it in the drum on purpose."

"I know a guy did that once," Nick said.

Elizabeth could do without his interruptions, but she wasn't about to tell him to shut up.

Marti straightened her shoulders more. "That's when I looked in the little window. And I saw…Louella Belle." She put her arms on the table and laid her head on them, sobbing. "I was so rude to her earlier."

Nick patted her shoulder and half shrugged to Elizabeth. "It'll be okay, Marti."

"No, it won't!"

Nick sat back, frowning and then raised his eyebrows at Elizabeth.

Elizabeth stood and walked the few steps to Marti's stool. "He means at some point you'll feel somewhat better." She nodded at Nick. "How about getting Marti some water, or a Dr. Pepper."

Marti sniffed into her arms. "Iced tea would be good."

Elizabeth tore a paper towel from the roll on the counter and placed one in front of Marti's arms, then touched her shoulder before moving back to her own stool. "When you feel you can, I'd like to continue."

Marti sniveled, sat up part way, and blew her nose. "I'm sorry."

"Not an I'm sorry thing," Elizabeth said.

Nick placed the glass of iced tea in front of Marti.

"Do we need to make more?" she sniffed.

Elizabeth smiled. "Tomorrow, I think."

"Oh, right." She blew her nose one more time, and took a sip of tea. She half-smiled at Nick. "Perfect amount of sugar. Thanks."

Elizabeth didn't want to hear about sugar in tea. "After you looked in the dryer, what did you do?"

"I screamed."

"A lot," Nick said. "At first I couldn't tell where the screaming was coming from."

Marti hugged herself. "I kept dropping my phone, but I finally got through to the 9-1-1 operator. I should have called the station, but I didn't know the number. The dispatcher man couldn't understand me."

"Always call 9-1-1," Elizabeth said. "They relay calls to us." She had already heard that the dispatcher had a tough time figuring out where to send anyone. Marti's garbled words initially sounded more like 'little bat' than 'laundromat.'

"So," Nick said, "I figured out who was screaming, and got there in like a minute. I mean, once I remembered where Marti'd gone."

Elizabeth hadn't realized Nick had run over. He must have gone back to the diner when her officers arrived. "Glad to hear it."

"And then, let's see. I know I was sitting on the floor, by the door, when Officer Grayson arrived. Oh, before that I stopped the dryer and opened the door. But I didn't, I didn't touch her."

"Good." Elizabeth realized her tone was more emphatic than needed, because Nick and Marti started. More quietly, she said, "Good judgment."

"And then, well, I told Officer Grayson some stuff, but I think I was kind of hard to understand, because it took a minute for him to get to look in the dryer."

Grayson's description of their early conversation had been, "Harried and hugely crying."

"And then he called more officers," Nick said. "When they got there, I left. Cause, you know, the diner was still open."

"Sure," Elizabeth said. "Did you give Grayson any information?"

Nick shook his head. "I told 'em I didn't look in the dryer, and only came over when Marti screamed."

"Did anyone else come by?" Elizabeth asked. "Did either of you see anyone on the street as you ran over?"

Nick shook his head. "Most businesses around here were already closed, you know? So Gene, he came over, but he had a guy getting' tattooed in the chair. He said you can stop by, but he doesn't think he knows anything."

Elizabeth couldn't help but wonder if the lack of attention had to do with holiday preparations away from the center of town, or more because of the victim. Plenty of people would wish Louella Belle gone. Probably not dead, but definitely gone.

ELIZABETH FINISHED TALKING TO Marti and Nick without learning more – no unknown person had been in the diner, nor had they paid attention to who went in and out of the laundromat before Marti returned for the tablecloths. They did say it was usually busiest Friday night and Saturday morning, when college students did laundry. Mostly older customers during the day.

Elizabeth knew she could get more general info from Squeaky and moved to the diner's customer area to sit in one of the red booths, across from him.

Squeaky's hands shook as he drank his cold coffee. He knew little about the afternoon's happenings in the laundromat. "I took over that space because the flower shop closed and it was vacant. I got a USDA guaranteed loan, so good interest, you know? I thought the laundry machines would kinda run themselves. Make a little money, but not have to be there, like I'm always at my dry cleaning place."

Elizabeth had forgotten that Squeaky talked in paragraphs. "Passive income, I think they call it. So you saw not one person in the laundromat in the late afternoon?"

I went out to my car to get something, and I saw Grace Whittle and Stanley Buttons in there. They live at the senior apartments."

"Could you hear them when they were in there?"

"I had my TV on at the cleaners. You know, I have that box thing, so I don't have to pay for cable. And since it's cold, my main door was shut. You know, sometimes I have it open and just the storm door shut."

"So, you didn't hear anything at all?"

Squeaky shook his head. "I got a bell on the front door at the laundromat, but it's just so people think I know they come in. I don't hear it when all the doors are shut."

"Do you hear the washers and dryers going?"

"Not so much. If I put my ear on the wall I kinda can feel a shake from the washers when they're spinning, you know at the end. But I don't do that regular." He sat down his cup. "I had too much of this black crap. Makes my stomach hurt."

As Elizabeth reached into her pocket, she glanced toward the swinging door that led to the kitchen. "I had planned to order Nick's chili, so I brought some Tums."

"Heh, heh." For a moment, Squeaky grinned. "He's a little better'n Ben, but not a lot."

CHAPTER FOUR

ELIZABETH GOT BACK TO the station at seven-thirty Monday evening. Knowing city officials or media might come by, she glanced behind the counter that separated the public seating area from the bullpen, such as it was.

A larger department would host a couple dozen desks. Logland's held five battered wood desks, plus the mail cubbyholes and Sgt. Hammer's work area of a newer desk and two tables. Given the season, a stuffed reindeer sat in one mail cubby and each desk had gold garland wrapped around its sides.

Neat enough for outsiders, she decided.

Her stomach had growled for an hour. The desk behind the customer counter held a stack of subs. She pulled a ten from her pocket, placed it next to the pile, and grabbed what seemed to be a chicken sub.

No one was in the open bullpen, so she raised her voice. "Anybody around?"

Mahan called, "In the break room."

They usually locked the front door to the station at seven thirty and didn't staff it overnight unless a festival or homecoming was underway. Elizabeth kept a patrol car on duty, but at night emergency calls routed to the county 9-1-1 call center.

The county dispatcher knew how to reach the Logland officer on patrol. Elizabeth thought they sometimes woke up Grayson after he pulled into a local park to watch for late-night speeders.

Since Elizabeth would work late, she planned to leave the station open a little longer tonight. Anxiety over Louella Belle's murder could mean more calls.

She took a bite of her sandwich as she walked to the break room, which doubled as the supply closet and copier work space. "You guys finish at the laundromat?"

"Tony's there, Grayson's back on patrol. Sgt. Hammer had a PTA meeting to go to, so I came back here." Mahan pointed at her sandwich. "Bought those."

"Thanks, I left money on Hammer's desk."

He flushed. "I didn't mean you should pay."

Elizabeth smiled and sat across from him. "I know that. You have any thoughts about Louella Belle?"

He nodded at the yellow pad in front of him. "I'm makin' a list, like you always say. Lots of people irritated with her, but I don't think people like Doc Vickers would off her."

She grinned briefly. "No, I don't think any pediatrician would do that. What the heck did she do to irritate the good doctor?"

"She made up a stack of half-page things that talked about not giving kids any starchy foods and sugar, or something like that." He stood. "Got one in the file we started. Be back."

As a former Chicago police officer, Elizabeth had been used to a more formal approach to crime solving than Logland's. At least more formal record keeping. The guys were thorough in whatever they did, but they didn't used to document most conversations.

Her thoughts went back to Louella Belle. She hadn't known the woman well. One day in Alice's bookstore Louella Belle had come at her waving a book called "Watch What You Eat." She wanted Elizabeth to let her give a talk to the eight Logland officers so they'd be in what she called "fighting shape."

Elizabeth had politely asked if Louella Belle would buy the books, since the police department was already slightly over budget. Nothing more came of it.

Mahan came back and placed the flyer in front of Elizabeth. In capped, bold print it said, "ARE YOU FEEDING POISON TO YOUR CHILDREN?"

The bullet points stated the sugar and fat content of several popular breakfast cereals, as well as macaroni and cheese and frozen French fries. The last point said, "STOP BEFORE YOUR CHILDREN BALLOON TO THIS."

'This' was a photo of two stocky children about ages eight and ten, a boy and a girl. Though their faces had been blurred, they sported Logland Elementary t-shirts. Elizabeth could not imagine their parents giving permission to use the picture. "Where did you get his?"

"She left some in the bookstore. Alice just dropped it off. Said it was too bad Louella Belle was killed, but if these were her kids, she'd want to go after her."

Elizabeth studied the flyer as she chewed. "You know the kids?"

"Hammer's going to ask around at PTA."

Elizabeth tapped the flyer. "I take it Doctor Vickers didn't want these in his office?"

Grayson sat down again and picked up his sandwich. "Nope. The second time, the doc told Louella Belle if she did it again, he'd call us."

"But it never came to that?"

"This was just a couple of weeks ago. Doubt she tried it again so soon."

Elizabeth shook her head slightly. "She was a smart woman. What do you suppose made her so...aggressive about her beliefs?"

Mahan shrugged. "Some people get religion, some get nutrition."

"That's good. I never heard that."

"Not original," Mahan said.

Someone came in the front door. Mahan began to rise, but Elizabeth motioned he should stay seated. "I bet it's Jerry Pew." She handed the flyer to Mahan. "Let's not release it unless somebody asks about it."

A man's voice called, "Chief Friedman?"

"Coming, Jerry." Elizabeth thought the editor cut a lot of corners on reporting, whether covering high school sports or a bunch of car break-ins. He irritated people beyond the police department, but she cut him some slack because he had to do most of the paper's reporting.

Jerry leaned on the counter.

"Hey, Jerry. Know anything?" she asked.

"Came by to ask you the same thing."

Elizabeth placed her elbows on the counter and faced him. "Haven't heard from Skelly. Nobody I talked to saw anything unusual. Until Marti found Louella Belle, of course."

"I been thinking she must have been in that dryer for a couple hours."

"Why do you say that?"

"Once it's dark, it's easy to see in that place. Daytime not so much." Jerry jabbed a finger toward Elizabeth. "Squeaky lets people put posters for bingo and stuff on his windows. You kind of have to peer around them to really see what's going on, but you can see in if you really look."

"Good point."

Jerry nodded. "I kinda stood outside, listening to folks while you were in there with her. Never heard so many people speak ill of the dead."

"Anyone seem especially angry with her?"

Jerry shook his head. "Mostly just tired of listening to her pet peeves for a lot of years. Kinda pushy, she was. Skelly didn't have any ideas about what killed her?"

Elizabeth shook her head. "Between part of her being wet and her time in the dryer, it's complicated."

"Huh. Didn't realize someone actually put her in there to dry."

"I, uh, doubt they did."

Since the laundromat had been in full view of anyone standing outside it for maybe half-an-hour after Marti's screams let everyone know she found Louella Belle, Elizabeth had decided to tell him more than she might have in different circumstances. He'd seen Louella Belle's body on the table before she and Grayson hung the paper on the glass.

"Cause of death is not obvious. We'll have to wait for Skelly to do his magic."

"Already had tomorrow's paper put to bed. I'll put something short on the web page."

Elizabeth avoided telling him she didn't care what he wrote. "Give me a call tomorrow."

She waited until Jerry was out the door before walking toward the break room. Her vibrating phone stopped her. "Chief Friedman here."

"Skelly here. Heard something from Dingle."

"You letting the city clerk help in the hospital's autopsy suite?"

"Suite, that's funny. He has a guilty conscience."

Elizabeth found it hard to imagine the usually pompous Dingle having any pangs of conscience. "Do tell."

"She'd been bugging him a lot at the office."

"Of course." Elizabeth could almost see Skelly smile.

"To get rid of her, Dingle told her he could use some help figuring out if anything weird was going on at the laundromat."

Elizabeth flushed, irritated. "He didn't mention anything to me."

"He didn't think anything was wrong, he just didn't like seeing a lot of college kids in and out of there. That's not how he put it of course."

"Exactly what did he say?" she asked.

"Dingle said he thought the college kids were using it more as a hang-out than a place to do laundry. His words were he 'wanted to know if they were up to something,' and he asked her to pay attention to the place."

Elizabeth sat on the edge of Hammer's desk. "That old fart wants to micro-manage my budget, but he can't be troubled to talk to me about something that bothered him."

Skelly's voice came in and out of the phone, as if he was doing something else while he talked to Elizabeth. "I don't think Dingle really was bothered, just wasn't something he could control, and he wanted her out of his office. Now he feels guilty."

"He should!"

Skelly sounded surprised. "Something was going on there?"

"No idea. But you put her in the mix and she'll annoy people enough to cause trouble."

"Maybe she did see something," Skelly offered.

Elizabeth sighed. "And God forbid she bring it to me if she could hassle someone on her own. Any thoughts on cause of death?"

"Sent some bloodwork to the lab, but doubt it'll show much. Besides the arm, her neck was partially broken. Enough to get her to pass out from pain if she hadn't already. But I can't tell if it's from before or after she took her ride."

"Okay. Talk to you tomorrow," she said.

"You eat yet?" Skelly asked.

"Mahan bought subs if you want to stop by. He just got them."

"I'll pass. Good night."

Elizabeth started for her office, where she knew Hammer would have placed a pile of messages for her. Her phone vibrated again. "Yes?"

"Chief, Grayson here."

"What's up?"

"Bike theft, so I'll take a report for a few minutes rather than patrol."

"Odd time of year for that. Kid's bikes?"

"Belonged to young teen, so not a big one."

The bike behind Gene's tattoo parlor flashed through her mind. "Damn. See if a bike is behind Gene's place, in the alley. Call me either way."

"Will do."

Elizabeth cursed herself. She may have walked right by the murderer's mode of getaway.

CHAPTER FIVE

MOST DAYS ELIZABETH WORE a blazer and slacks, maybe a suit if she had to go to a budget meeting or talk to the mayor. The Tuesday morning after Louella Belle's murder, she figured media – more serious media than Jerry Pew – might stop by, so she wore her formal chief's uniform. She didn't realize she'd left the jacket across the bottom of her bed for a few minutes when she'd last worn it, and had to use lots of scotch tape to get all the cat hair off.

Elizabeth carried her flat, official hat under her arm as she arrived at the station at seven-thirty. She felt well-rested considering the evening's events. She'd even stopped by Casey's for a bag of mini-bagels for her officers.

Sgt. Hammer had beaten her in, apologetic for having left on time the day before. "My wife did the last two middle-school PTA meetings. She understands me changing plans when there's an emergency, but…" He did a palms-up shrug. "Louella Belle was already dead."

"We had plenty of guys around. Grayson said you were going to see if anyone knew the kids on the flyer."

Hammer began to clear off the wrappers from the prior night's sub sandwiches. He didn't like it when his desk became a catch-all. "Thing is, Chief, lots of folks saw the picture. A few people had heard about Louella Belle's death and a couple parents had the flyer and showed it around. Instead of asking them about it straight-away I figured I'd listen for a few minutes."

Elizabeth grinned. "Not like anyone could escape the meeting early."

Hammer swept the remaining crumbs from his desk into the trash can that sat behind it. "The December meeting's part social, so folks don't rush out. I heard pretty quickly that the kids on the flyer not only attend school there, they're the assistant principal's son and daughter."

Elizabeth slapped herself in the forehead. "What could Louella Belle have been thinking?"

Hammer shrugged. "Happy to say I don't know how her mind worked. My guess is she wanted people talking about the picture. My son's science teacher is a friend. At the end, I asked him what he'd heard."

"And?"

"You know the assistant principal? Her name's Avery Maxwell. She just saw it a couple days ago, and he said she hit the ceiling. Called a lawyer and everything."

"There's somebody else to interview," Elizabeth said.

"Yeah, well, I wouldn't start out by asking her where she was yesterday at four o'clock or whenever. She has a short fuse."

"I'll light it if it gets some good info. I'm going to check my desk for messages to see if Grayson left a note about a bicycle I saw behind Gene's last night. If I'm on the phone, interrupt me if Skelly calls, would you?"

"Will do, and he did."

"Called?" Elizabeth asked.

"I meant Grayson left you a note."

Since Hammer said nothing more, Elizabeth left him to enter data from the officers' time sheets so the city would know how many hours each man booked.

Three minutes later, she wished Grayson's message had been different. As he finished the report on the teen's stolen bicycle, Finn Clancy had called to say his bike had been stolen.

When Grayson checked the alley behind Man Up Tattoos, he found no bike. Gene didn't know one had been parked there.

Instinct told Elizabeth that the killer hadn't wanted to call attention to him or herself by riding away on the likely stolen bike. He probably went back when the police had left.

Final Cycle

Had the bicycle thief taken it earlier in the day? Elizabeth thumbed through the short stack of incident reports beneath Grayson's note. The top one was Calderone's report on Louella Belle, the second Grayson's reports on the two bikes. Stapled to it was a photo of a rusty men's bike with its scruffy owner sitting on it. Definitely the one Elizabeth had seen behind Gene's. Grayson's note that said Clancy had provided the photo.

"Nuts." A glance at the bottom of the report revealed Finn Clancy's phone number. "Too bad if it's too early." She dialed.

A man barked into the phone. "This better be damn important!"

"Chief Friedman here, and it is, Mr. Clancy. Thanks for picking up."

More quietly, he asked, "Find my bike? Heard you saw it and let somebody ride off with it."

"Unfortunately, we didn't have your stolen property report when I walked down the alley."

Clancy said nothing. Elizabeth knew Finn Clancy as a man who preferred to lounge around town complaining about having no job. She had also heard that the owner of the twenty-four-hour gas station on the edge of town had offered him work stocking shelves at night, with the possibility of a cashier's job if things worked out. Clancy had told him he didn't work well after dark.

"So, you gonna get it back? That's my main transportation you know."

"I can appreciate that. It would help to know when you last had it and when you noticed it missing."

"I told all that to the Grayson guy."

She nodded. "I have the report. I would like to hear it directly from you."

Clancy launched into a long-winded tale of putting his bike in the rack near Doris Minx's cookie shop, and then heading to the dollar store to do some Christmas shopping. After going to Dollar General, he had dinner at the Weed 'n Feed and walked back to Doris' place about seven-thirty. No bike. "And it took your guy a damn long time to come take my report."

"I'm sorry. You may have heard we were investigating Louella Belle Simpson's murder."

Less boisterously, he said, "Oh, yeah, well, that's all right. You gonna find it?"

"I hope so. As Officer Grayson seems to have told you, I think I saw it behind Man Up Tattoos, in the alley. You're sure you didn't leave it there?"

"Damn sure."

"And no lock on it when it was in the bike rack?" she asked.

"Does it matter?"

Elizabeth almost snapped back at him, but held back. "If someone used bolt cutters to get at it, I'd be inclined to think the person regularly stole bikes or other locked items. If no lock, it could have been taken impulsively."

"Yeah, well, no lock."

"We'll keep looking. I have to tell you something really important."

"What's that?"

"If you find it, don't touch it. We'll want to check it for prints."

His laugh was course. "It ain't all that important."

"Not to you, maybe. But it was near the site of a murder. I want to know who touched it besides you."

SKELLY CALLED AT ELEVEN Tuesday morning. "Not a lot more to tell you. My guess would be someone shoved Louella Belle and she fell against a thin pipe or something like that. Injured her neck enough that she probably passed out."

"Could it have been the lip of the laundry tub?"

"Might make sense. She might not have died right away, but it would have been quick. They could have hefted her up and put her head under water until she stopped breathing."

Elizabeth groaned. "That poor woman."

"Doubt she knew what was going on. Just the smallest amount of water in her lungs. She wasn't gulping for air."

She sighed. "The guys got about forty different sets of latent prints from the place. I guess we'll focus first on those around the tub."

"Not the dryer, Chief?"

She smiled. "The dryer, too. But by the time they got her over there the killers could have thought to put on gloves. Cold enough that just about everyone would have had a pair with them last night."

"Good point. That's why you're the big boss. Gotta run."

Elizabeth had wanted to ask if he had results of any blood work, but she supposed he would have said so. He'd likely have a written preliminary report to her in a few hours.

She studied a list of people to interview. It included anyone Nick and Marti could remember being in the diner between the time Louella Belle left and was found dead, and businesses near the laundromat. She added Assistant Principal Maxwell, the city clerk, and Louella Belle's neighbors.

She'd asked Mahan to visit nearby gas stations to see if any patrons seemed to be acting odd in the late afternoon or early evening, or had wet sleeves – a sign they may have dealt with Louella Belle in the laundromat.

Squeaky said he would develop a list of regular weekday laundromat customers. The few he'd remembered either lived in the senior housing apartments or worked in a couple nearby businesses. Elizabeth hoped he could come up with a more diverse group.

Before she looked at anyone else, she called Donald Dingle.

If someone could have a guilty tone of voice, the city clerk did. "You heard about me asking Louella Belle to, uh, stay alert?"

Elizabeth didn't plan to cut him any slack. "You told her you thought students used the laundromat for more than washing clothes, and asked her to check it out."

Dingle's usual officious tone came through. "Now, chief, that's an exaggeration."

"Glad to hear it. What did you ask her to do?"

Dingle said nothing for several seconds. "See, I saw a lot of them going in and out of there."

"The students, you mean?"

"Yes. It seemed odd. I mean, they have washers and dryers in the dorms."

Elizabeth rolled her eyes. "Kids like to congregate. Did you think something illegal was going on at the laundromat?"

Dingle spoke forcefully. "How would I know without information?"

"The police work for the city. Why ask Louella Belle rather than me? Has it occurred to you that you may have placed her in danger?"

"Now, Chief, you have no proof of that."

Elizabeth deliberately said nothing.

"Do you?"

"You know I don't discuss active investigations. Have you asked private citizens to snoop anywhere else on your behalf?" Elizabeth knew it might not be smart to antagonize Dingle, but she wanted to be sure he wouldn't do something stupid again. At least not in the same way.

After at least ten seconds, a subdued Dingle said, "No."

"Did Louella Belle pass on any of her observations?"

"Not that I recall," Dingle said.

"Okay. Next time contact me, please."

"I'm getting another call. I have to go." Dingle hung up.

Calderone walked in. "Heard who you were talking to. Skelly told me what Dingle said about Louella Belle."

Elizabeth shoved her office phone a few inches from her. "He's an old fool in a position where he can do harm. If I find out she was killed 'looking into things,' I'm going to talk to the county attorney to see if any charge would apply to Dingle."

"Damn, Chief, remind me not to piss you off."

CHAPTER SIX

ELIZABETH DIDN'T OFTEN ASK her officers to work during meal breaks, but the day after a murder was an exception. She scheduled lunch in her office to go over what they knew, and ordered in pizza and pre-packaged salads from the Logland Pizza Parlor next to Alice's bookstore.

"Whadda we owe you?" Mahan asked.

"Merry Christmas," she said.

"In that case," Calderone said, "you should have ordered a supreme."

"Damn, Tony," Hammer said.

Elizabeth pointed a fork at Calderone. "Next time you buy."

Mahan laughed. "That'll teach you."

Officer Taylor ate quietly, as usual. After all the school shootings around the country, she'd assigned him to be a school resource officer. He wasn't stationed at any of the three schools, but he spent much time at one or the other, mostly working on preparedness and getting to know the teachers and some of the kids. He largely kept in touch through Sergeant Hammer and came into the station at the beginning and end of his shifts.

School was out and Taylor had taken a few days off. He'd volunteered to come in, so Elizabeth had him attend the meeting to add what he could and maybe do some interviews later. Tall and red-haired, he couldn't be assigned to anything that required blending in.

They ate quietly for a couple of minutes before Elizabeth said, "I wanted to compare what we've done so far so we're all on the same page. We need to be anyway, but I've already had calls from a TV station in Springfield and papers in other parts of the county. We're lucky it's been icy, or our media friends would have already stopped by."

Hammer put a short list on the table. "This is who we interviewed so far. Tony has some ideas on who else to talk to."

Hammer's list included Nick and Marti, Dingle, Mayor Humphrey, Jerry Pew, Squeaky, Doris, and several other local business owners. None of the latter had been open when Marti found Louella Bella.

"And I checked with Doris, like you asked," Calderone said, "Louella Belle didn't stop by there for a free sugar cookie."

"I talked to people at PTA, made a few notes," Hammer said. "But these were conversations last night, they weren't full interviews. We'll have to talk to the middle school Assistant Principal, Avery Maxwell."

Elizabeth nodded to Taylor. "You have a good relationship with her?"

He nodded. "When I stopped by her office a few days ago, she told me about the flyer Louella Belle made with her kids' pictures."

"Angry, I take it?" Elizabeth asked.

"As a bee in a hot car. Said she and her husband were going to talk to a lawyer."

"Do you see her being angry enough to shove Louella Belle into the laundry tub and stuff her in the dryer?"

"No, mostly because I don't see her even finding Louella Belle to talk to her about it. Mrs. Maxwell might argue on a debate team, but she's kind of…snobby. She'd leave it to the lawyer."

"Okay, but when you talk to her, find out where she was late yesterday afternoon."

He nodded. "And her husband."

"Good point." Elizabeth pointed to Hammer's list of people interviewed. "Most of those on this list would have been pretty short conversations, at least any I did were. Except Marti."

Mahan nodded. "Like Doris Minx. She said she didn't know anything except Louella Belle left the diner mad. She did say when Louella Belle stormed out there was a young couple with a couple kids at one of the booths. Don't know names."

"Marti or Nick might," Calderone said. "I figure we need to talk a few other regular laundromat customers. Squeaky didn't know a lot of names, but he mentioned a couple folks from the senior center and the college guys they call Herbie Hiccup and Just Juice Jenson. Maybe Finn Clancy again about his bike."

"Hammer told me yesterday that no one in the school system knew whether Louella Belle had any relatives." Elizabeth said.

"That really sucks," Mahan said. "Plus, Skelly's concerned he'll be ready to release the body, and no one's said they'll claim it."

"Damn," Elizabeth said. "Did she have an attorney?"

Calderone flipped pages in his notebook. "She had a will done with the same lawyer Ben had his with, John Stone. He won't release it until he files it at the courthouse, but he said no individual benefitted from her death."

"What the heck does that mean?" Elizabeth asked.

"He wouldn't say which ones, but she left her money to organizations."

Elizabeth looked at Calderone. "Why Finn Clancy again?"

"Because he's a creep."

Hammer nodded. "Times two."

"Good as any criteria, I guess." Elizabeth said, dryly. "I don't know him well. Is he a native?"

Hammer said, "I know he graduated from high school here. Parents were sort of well off, but left most of what they had to a sister, or something like that. Guess they knew he'd blow it."

"You have more on his bike?" Elizabeth asked.

Mahan snorted. "Probably in a ditch somewhere. Not like anyone would steal it to use as a Christmas gift."

"Keep looking," Elizabeth said. "He told me he'd left the bike at Doris' place, then went to Dollar General, then Weed n' Feed. Follow up. Who checked the gas station by the highway?"

"I did," Calderone said. "No one looked hinky, nobody seemed to have wet gloves or jackets."

"Too bad," Elizabeth said. "When do we get any fingerprint results?"

"Tony gets an A for extra work," Mahan said.

Calderone shifted in his chair. "With Mahan's help, I lifted what I think are forty-two possible usable latent fingerprints. From the dryers, change machine, washing machines, and the laundry tub. No idea how many people that represents."

"Not that I question what you found," Elizabeth said, "but I thought there would be more."

"Yeah, lots of smeared prints, not even what you'd call partials," Calderone said. "We need enough of a print, preferably a couple fingers, to submit to the Automated Fingerprint ID system. I sent what we got to the state police yesterday. Will take at least a few days, especially because of the holiday."

Elizabeth frowned. "AFIS takes that long for a murder investigation?"

"It's because we have so many, and we didn't target any as probable suspects. If we had one set, or two, I could push them harder. Takes time to do the comparisons."

Elizabeth waved a hand. "Okay, I get it." But she mostly didn't. Maybe an elderly woman in a laundromat wasn't enough of a high-profile case for expediting the response. It should be.

"The thing is," Calderone said, "there's something like three million records in the Illinois database, more in the national one, of course. A lot of people who go into that laundromat would never have had their prints submitted for anything. Bet we don't get five hits."

AFTER LUNCH TUESDAY, ELIZABETH stopped by the senior apartments to meet with Grace Whittle and Stanley Buttons, two people Squeaky had named. She had called ahead, so when she entered they sat together on the vinyl sofa in the apartment's huge foyer. Elizabeth immediately thought of the poem, "Jack Spratt could eat no fat, his wife could eat no lean. And so between them both, you see, they licked the platter clean."

Canes rested near both of them, though Stanley Buttons certainly looked able-bodied. The round-faced Grace Whittle could have been a before picture for a weight loss commercial.

"You know about Louella Belle's murder, so you've probably figured out why I want to talk to you."

Grace shook her head slightly. "She wasn't in the laundromat when we were yesterday."

"When did you get there?" Elizabeth asked.

Stanley closed his eyes, concentrating. "Grace and I got there about two-fifteen."

Her eyes brightened. "We usually ride back together, but my daughter picked me up. I left first, about four. Just getting dark. That leaves Stanley without an alibi."

Elizabeth smiled briefly. "I don't think he's quite strong enough to have hurt Louella Belle."

Grace frowned. "Of course. Sorry to be flippant."

"What time did you leave, Mr. Buttons?"

"I'd say about four-fifteen. You know what time she got killed?"

"Looks like late afternoon or early evening," Elizabeth said, "but Dr. Hutton hasn't completed the full autopsy."

Stanley cleared his throat. "I told my son, up in Peoria. He wants to know how much I missed the killer by. You know, an hour? More? Less?"

"Toxicology reports can take more than a month," Grace said.

"Except on CSI," Stanley added.

Elizabeth smiled. "Isn't there a laundry room in this building? Seems a seven-story apartment would have at least one."

"In the basement," Stanley said.

Grace nodded. "But it's so much more pleasant at Squeaky's new place. And it's not so much walking."

"What do you mean?"

Stanley leaned forward. "Here, we take the elevator to the basement, then walk to the far side of the building. That's a long way to haul clothes. If we go to Squeaky's place, I pull up to the door of this building, Grace and I put the laundry in my back seat, and when we get to the laundromat we can use a cart to wheel the stuff around."

"Good to know. How about other times you were there. Did anyone you saw make you concerned for your safety?"

Grace shook her head. "Not me. You go sometimes when I don't, Stanley."

"Yes. I don't know everyone I see there. Not that the place is ever truly crowded. Usually one or two other people."

"People you know?" Elizabeth asked.

Stanley slowly shook his head. "I see some of the same people. Couple of students. Oh, Gene sometimes puts in laundry and comes in to check."

"I folded it for him once," Grace said.

Elizabeth nodded at her, then studied Stanley. He had again briefly shut his eyes as if concentrating, but didn't add anything else.

Elizabeth pulled out two of her cards. "If you think of anything else relevant, call the station, please."

As she left, Elizabeth heard Grace say, "This is exciting." She didn't seem to focus on the fact that a woman had died a violent death.

CHAPTER SEVEN

ELIZABETH HAD JUST STARTED her car when her phone buzzed. She glanced at caller ID. "Nuts." She pushed answer. "Officer Kermit. How go things in college security?" Elizabeth could envision the bobbing head of college security officer Walter, a.k.a. Wally, Kermit.

"Almost all the students went home for Christmas yesterday. We do more patrols, keep out lawbreakers. But it's quiet. Heard you had a murder."

"Yes, very sad. Did you know Louella Belle Simpson? She used to teach at the high school."

"Had her for consumer sciences about fifteen years ago. She made all us boys learn about nutrition and cooking. Used to be just the girls had to do that. Sorry to hear about her."

Elizabeth realized it was the closest to sorrow she had heard expressed. People said Louella Belle's death was a surprise or a shame. No one else had said they were sorry. "Did you keep in touch with her much?"

"Nope. You know how she was. Not a bad lady, but talked your ear off."

"Can I help you with anything, Wally?" Elizabeth dug an earbud from her pocket so she could drive.

"Seeins' how it's quiet at Sweat…I mean here at Southern Illinois Agricultural College, I wondered if you might need some help."

Elizabeth wasn't likely to ask a man who ate powdered donuts at a prior crime scene for help. "We can always use more listening posts. Were you downtown yesterday, or have you heard anyone talking about Louella Belle lately?"

"Most people want to forget her."

Elizabeth laughed, the first time in more than a day. "I didn't know her well, but I've heard that. When's the last time you saw her?"

"Grocery store last week. She said I didn't have enough fresh vegetables in my cart, then she told this lady she shouldn't be buying sugar cereal for her kids. Made the kid cry, a little boy."

"Jeez."

"Yeah, manager came right over. Told her to remember what he said. Don't know what he meant, but I figured it meant not to bother other customers."

"Huh." Elizabeth figured she should talk to the grocery store manager. "You ever go in the laundromat?"

"Nah. Once I got the teaching job, too, I bought a little house. Real nice, edge of town, near the Logland water tower."

Elizabeth had forgotten that Wally also taught chemistry part-time. "Great. Listen, Wally…"

"So, I got a couple days off around Christmas. I could, you know, ask around for you."

She spoke firmly. "No, thanks. But I'm always open…You know, there might be one thing."

"At your service, Chief Friedman!"

"Near the laundromat I saw a rusty men's bike. Turns out it had been reported stolen. When we checked back, it was gone."

"So, you think the perp owned it?" Wally asked.

"Probably didn't belong to the murderer. Someone else reported it stolen, but the killer could have used it. Can you keep your eyes open on campus? If you see an older bike in an unexpected place, I'd like to hear about it."

Excitement dripped from Wally's words. "I'll call you personally, Chief. I still have your cell number."

Elizabeth wished he didn't. "That's fine, but if you don't get me, don't wait. Call the station."

"I'm on it!"

"If you find the bike, please don't touch it. Just call."

"Ten-four." Wally hung up.

Elizabeth already regretted the request.

Final Cycle

BACK AT THE STATION THAT Tuesday afternoon, Elizabeth went over her list to decide who to talk to next. She did not appreciate the prospect of calling Assistant Principal Avery Maxwell. The topic would be tough – Louella Belle had used a photo of her young children in her misguided approach to address childhood obesity.

In the lunch meeting, Taylor said the assistant principal had planned to contact a lawyer about Louella Belle's flyer, and earlier Hammer said he thought she had. Elizabeth had no desire to be quizzed about whether Louella Belle's estate could be sued.

She'd let Taylor try Maxwell first, and then decide if she had to follow up.

Elizabeth usually remembered names, but when Sweathog students were called Just Juice Jenson and Herbie Hiccup, she remembered their nicknames better. She asked Hammer to find out if they were still in town.

He reported that they were but hadn't seemed anxious to come to the station. He told them the choice was come to the station or have an officer visit their apartment. They agreed to come down to the station within the hour.

As Hammer ushered them into chairs opposite her desk, Elizabeth thought the two men appeared nervous. Or maybe they usually didn't meet an interviewer's eyes and often wiped sweaty palms on their jeans.

"Thanks for coming in guys. Glad you haven't left for home yet."

"No problem, Chief," Just Juice said. "We're stayin' here for Christmas."

"Yeah, not sure we know much we can help you, but we'll try," Herbie said. "Going home for New Year's Eve."

Most young people would have done the opposite, but Elizabeth didn't pursue that point. Instead, she let her gaze travel between them. "The diner is across from the laundromat. Doris Minx mentioned that she thought you were doing laundry not long before Marti found Louella Belle."

They nodded in tandem. "Doin' laundry," Herbie said.

"Anyone else in there when you were?" she asked.

Just Juice adopted a pose of concentration. "An old guy left as we came in. Maybe four-fifteen or so."

Elizabeth nodded. "I think I know who that was."

"Only other person was the guy who works in Dollar General." Herbie nodded. "You know, used to be the fraternity president at the college, but he got kicked out."

Elizabeth knew Blake Wessley better than she would have liked. Good looking and arrogant, having to work at DG, as the locals called the store, would have been quite a few pegs below where he thought he should be on life's pecking order.

"Doing his laundry, too?" she asked.

Just Juice sat forward in his chair. "He separates it like my mom does. You know, by colors."

Elizabeth kept her face expressionless. "Some people do that. Did you guys talk to him?"

"Not really," Herbie said. "We were gettin' ready to leave, so it was maybe 5:00. Dark already."

"We're coming up on the shortest day of the year," Elizabeth said. "Listen, besides this horrible thing with Louella Belle, do you know of any other funny business going on in the laundromat?"

They looked at each other and back at her. "Like what?" Herbie asked.

She smiled. "I'm asking you. Did you ever see anything odd?"

Just Juice shrugged. "When his clothes are in the washer, Finn Clancy sleeps in a corner, in his underwear."

Elizabeth sat up straighter. "He what?"

"But under a blanket," Herbie added. "You know, one of those gray ones they give out at the Mission."

"Does he bother anyone?"

Just Juice grinned. "He snores pretty loud."

Elizabeth had been thinking more on the order of women being frightened by seeing a man in his underwear. Might not be illegal, but she'd have to talk to Squeaky about it. He could tell Clancy the laundromat dress code included at least pants and a t-shirt.

"Um," Herbie said. "He maybe mostly does it when it's only men."

"How would he know when that would be?" Elizabeth asked.

Final Cycle

"So, it closes at ten," Just Juice said, "but women don't go there much after dark. It's, well, you know, dark."

"Any particular reason to avoid the place?" she asked.

"Kinda lonely downtown then. Nothin' open. But," he shrugged, "not like Clancy would bother anyone."

Unless Louella Belle bugged him, too. She looked from one man to the other. "Why did you say you two aren't going home for the holidays?"

Herbie leaned back more in his chair. "My folks are visiting my mom's family in Arizona."

"I might go home for New Year's," Just Juice said. "I got a lot of studying to do. I'm kinda on probation. With my parents, not the school."

Elizabeth smiled. "Marti and Nick have a good lunch on Christmas Eve."

Both nodded. "Turkey with all the trimmings," Herbie said.

After the two men left, Elizabeth made notes on the conversation and reread them. Knowing they had been in the laundromat at five P.M. helped with a timeline. But they had been nervous about something.

Herbie and Just Juice were older than some other students, probably on the so-called five-year plan to prolong college. Maybe they funded their constant meals at the diner by selling something at the laundromat. It didn't have to be drugs, it could be exam questions or cigarettes they obtained cheaply.

She called Squeaky at the dry cleaner's. "Mr. Miller. You doing better today?"

Squeaky's sigh came through the phone. "I suppose. Feel bad Louella Belle got killed in my business. Maybe if I never opened it she'd be alive."

There it was again. Someone felt bad, but had nothing effusive, or even nice, to say about her. "We haven't come up with much, so I thought I'd see if you had any more thoughts about whether her death could relate to the laundromat, or if she happened to be in the wrong place at the wrong time."

"I didn't even know she went in there. She had a house not too far from the college."

"Right. How about any funny business not connected with Louella Belle. Any noise complaints, any machines damaged?"

"No." Squeaky paused for a couple of seconds. "But now you mention it, I wondered a couple times if someone was trying to get into the change machine. I'm not as careful as I could be with change and stuff."

"What do you mean?" Elizabeth asked.

"Well, a couple times the bills that came in didn't seem to jive with the change that went out." He paused. "Or maybe it was the other way around."

Elizabeth felt like asking him if he'd already had a couple of beers. "So maybe someone took out some bills that had been inserted for change?"

"Might could be. I'm not sure."

"You mind if we look at the bill changer?"

"Sure. Stop by for the key."

She smiled slightly to herself, envisioning the rectangular machine that hung on the wall. It had to be bolted on well, if it held a lot of quarters. "Just the outside. I'll have a look at the lock and maybe see if there are some scratches near it."

"Huh. Good idea. Hey, um, I don't mean no disrespect, but when can I reopen the laundry?"

"We're pretty much done. I'll have the guys take down the crime scene tape in about an hour."

Squeaky said a doleful goodbye.

Elizabeth buzzed Hammer. "We have a key to Squeaky's laundromat, right?"

"Yep, in the small safe in the locker room."

"Squeaky doesn't know about any funny business, but he wonders if the change that went out of the bill changer is the same as the money that went in."

Hammer grunted. "Squeaky's not so good at math after noon."

"So I hear. You, or one of the others, have a look at the machine. He's willing to give us the key, but I'd like your opinion on whether the lock looks like it's been tampered with."

"Sure, chief. Me or Calderone, maybe Mahan, we'll check it out."

She relayed what Herbie and Just Juice had told her about timing and who else they saw in the laundromat at times. "I'd rather not sound out Finn Clancy about his sleeping habits. Why don't you talk to Squeaky about it, and then Clancy."

"Jeez Louise." Hammer chuckled. "Can we make Grayson talk to him?"

"Why Grayson?" Elizabeth asked.

"It'll wake him up if he has to find Finn Clancy under a blanket."

CHAPTER EIGHT

WEDNESDAY MORNING, ELIZABETH decided to first tackle Blake Wessley, former president of the college fraternity. Shenanigans at the one Greek house on campus had led the college to shutter it. He'd lost his campus residence and, from Wessley's perspective, probably a lot of stature.

Elizabeth herself had asked the college's president not to expel the students. She didn't condone their actions, but eighteen-to-twenty-year olds could be stupid in groups. Expulsion could ruin lives.

She had suggested that President Dodd require them to maintain a certain grade point and perform community service in town, or tutoring on campus. Though she figured several of the regular beer imbibers would need the extra instruction rather than be able give it.

Dodd let them stay, but took away any scholarships. Elizabeth did not accept his offer to have some frat brothers volunteer at the police station.

Hammer told her Blake Wessley was to be at Dollar General at one-thirty that afternoon, and Elizabeth asked the manager if she could stop by to see if he could help in the investigation.

"You won't have sirens or anything, will you?"

Elizabeth smiled into the phone. Matt Howard was perpetually nervous. As he walked through the store, he straightened any shelf he passed. "No, and if Mr. Wessley is with a customer I won't interrupt. I just have a couple questions about what he saw in the laundromat the other day."

"Ah, yes. Poor Louella Belle," Howard said.

"Did you know her well, or see her that afternoon?"

"No on both counts. In fact, I had to ask her not to talk to other customers last Halloween season. She harassed people buying bags of candy. Told one woman she knew the candy wasn't for trick or treaters. You can imagine how irritated customers were."

Elizabeth held in a laugh. "Food police are never popular."

She had just hung up her phone when Hammer poked his head into her office. "Taylor called. Said that assistant principal told him she doesn't have time to talk to him before Christmas."

Elizabeth raised her hands in a 'what-are-we-going-to-do' gesture. "Well, I guess she told us. We can just rearrange our murder investigation."

Hammer laughed. "Milder than I thought you'd be."

"Call her back. Tell her I'm interviewing her personally. We can do it at her house or here at the station. I can have someone pick her up. Ten-thirty works for me, but if she can't do it then, let her pick the time."

Elizabeth pulled out her notebook and jotted a couple questions for Maxwell on the last page.

Hammer walked back in less than a minute. "That Maxwell woman doesn't want to meet you here."

"Sheesh. Does she want me to come to her place?"

Hammer's look conveyed annoyance. "I suggested the Bully Pulpit, but she said she doesn't go there. She said Doris Minx's bakery would be an appropriate location."

"Still ten-thirty?"

"She didn't say different." Hammer turned to go back to the bullpen.

A glance at her office clock told Elizabeth it was only nine-forty-five. She grabbed another cup of coffee from the break room and returned to her desk to go over last night's incident reports.

Two unlocked cars had been relieved of the small amounts of money in their glove boxes and change holders, and an elderly man had skidded into the fire hydrant in front of the library. "Bummer," she said aloud.

She stopped casual reading at the next report. Two bicycles had been stolen, one from a house not far from the college, another in her own neighborhood. Both men's bikes, one quite new. Aside from brief descriptions of the bikes and the times their owners noticed they had disappeared -- about ten PM, when they were locking their garages -- the reports had few details.

She buzzed Hammer. "Any more on the two new bicycle thefts?"

"No. Different parts of town. But I'm sure you noticed that."

"Other than Finn Cassidy's bike and one other being stolen two nights ago, how often would you say bikes get stolen?"

Hammer didn't hesitate. "Around town, just a few times a year, always in summer."

"What do you make of it?"

Elizabeth could envision his typical shrug. "Too cold to ride around on one. Or too slippery, anyway."

"You think a killer is trying to confuse us?"

"Probably," Hammer said. "That's what I'd do."

She smiled. "Remind me to check your behavior next time you go off somewhere." She hung up. After she talked to Assistant Principal Avery, she'd drive by the two locations to see if anything about the homes or locales seemed to tie them together.

She finished her coffee in two gulps and moved to her file cabinet, where she put her gun when she was in the office. She removed the Glock and holstered it under her heavy jacket. Doris wouldn't appreciate having someone interviewed in her bakery-coffee shop combo. She'd keep her gun out of sight.

AVERY MAXWELL HAD ARRIVED at Doris Minx's coffee shop before Elizabeth. She wore an expensive-looking ski jacket with what seemed to be real fur rimming the hood. She sat so straight against the small chair's curly-Q back that just seeing her made Elizabeth's spine ache.

Doris called from behind the glass-enclosed bakery counter. "Black, Elizabeth?"

"How about hot tea? I've had too much coffee already."

Final Cycle

"Sure thing." Doris walked to the far side of the counter and busied herself with a mug.

Elizabeth took a chair opposite Avery Maxwell. "Thanks for meeting me."

Her strident tone matched her posture. "This is very inconvenient, Chief Friedman. It's three days before…"

"Murder is inconvenient, too, Mrs. Maxwell. I'd love to have someone behind bars before Christmas."

Maxwell stared at her. "Very well. I can't imagine I know anything that will help you."

Elizabeth put her notebook on the table. "Let's find out. When was the last time you, personally, saw Louella Belle Simpson?"

Maxwell tossed her perfectly styled blonde hair. "I saw her from a distance in the grocery store a few days ago. I doubt she saw me, or she would have harassed me."

"Had you already seen that flyer with the photo of your children?"

Maxwell flushed. "I can assure you not. Do you have any idea what that did to my children's self-esteem?"

"It was a terrible thing to do. If she were alive, I'd pull her into the station for a serious conversation."

Maxwell's tight expression loosened somewhat. "We spoke to a lawyer, but then…well, he says it doesn't matter now."

Elizabeth decided to become Avery Maxwell's friend, at least for a minute. "Perhaps not legally, but I'm sorry your kids were embarrassed."

"Thank you."

"When was the last time you spoke to Louella Belle? Did she give you any indication she didn't like aspects of, I'm not sure what to call it, your family's nutrition decisions?"

Doris Minx brought Elizabeth's hot tea and a cup of ice water for Maxwell. "I know you said you didn't want anything, but I hated to see the chief drink alone."

Elizabeth smiled. "Thanks, Doris."

Maxwell simply nodded.

Doris' usually friendly expression darkened for a moment, and she turned toward her counter and walked away.

"Mrs. Maxwell?" Elizabeth said.

"She used to come into the building every couple of weeks and visit with the kitchen staff. She saw herself as some sort of Heloise of the kitchen, and dispensed a lot of unwanted advice."

Elizabeth shook her head slightly. "I've been the recipient of her ideas."

"Then you know how annoying she could be. Because she was a school system retiree and helped at that summer lunch program for children, we let her in with no appointment. But a couple of times Principal Henry told her not to wander the halls."

"I'm a little surprised. Aren't your doors locked these days?"

Maxwell nodded. "Yes. Frankly, letting her in was easier than having her throw a tantrum." When Elizabeth raised her eyebrows, she added, "Some of the kids even liked her. I guess because of the summer lunch. And the last couple of years she brought seed packets to give to the fifth grade. In the spring."

"Seed packets?"

"Yes. For beans, I think. Organic. She was big on that."

Elizabeth jotted a couple of lines in her notebook. "The more we know about her behavior the better. So, you last talked to her at the middle school?"

"But just for a second. She tried to corral me, maybe three weeks ago. Our secretary explained I was leaving for a meeting with the school board budget committee. Louella Belle tried to follow me to my car, but I told her I was too busy to talk."

"Do you know what she wanted?"

Maxwell shook her head, frowning. "No, but I wonder if she put the children's picture on that flyer to get back at me."

"A mean thing to do," Elizabeth said. "You didn't personally talk to her after you saw the flyer?"

She shook her head emphatically. "If I had been in the same room with her I would have tried to strangle her. I called our lawyer."

Elizabeth smiled. "You'll be happy to know she wasn't strangled."

Maxwell flushed and lowered her chin slightly.

"You probably know she died in the late afternoon on Monday Where were you about that time?"

Maxwell's chin came up sharply and she glared at Elizabeth. "How dare you accuse me of…"

Final Cycle

Elizabeth moved her hand, palm flat, in a downward motion. "I'm asking a question."

"But why would you even ask?"

"While you would be a very unlikely suspect, you have very good reason to be furious with her for a very personal reason."

Maxwell took a sip of her water. "Monday was the last day of class before the holiday. The building quiets when the children leave the building. A couple of teachers stopped by to say Merry Christmas, one to talk about a child she thought might not be getting enough food at home."

Elizabeth wondered what the school did in a case like that, but instead she asked, "And I won't trouble these teachers unless I have a reason to later, but I would like their names."

"Annette Chesney, fourth grade, and Dick Plummer, second."

"And if I may ask, how do you figure out if a family has food? Call Social Services?"

She shook her head. "We want families to trust us, and there's a stigma to involving Social Services. The food pantry gives us vouchers, extras this time of year. It lets families who haven't gone there know they can."

"How do you get the voucher to them?"

"Depends on what we know about the family situation. It would take a few minutes to outline the options."

"Right." Elizabeth closed her notebook. "Can you think of anyone as angry, or more so, with Louella Belle than you?"

Maxwell smiled for the first time. "How long do you have?"

CHAPTER NINE

DESPITE THE ASSISTANT PRINCIPAL'S hint of potential suspects, the situations she described were similar to others Elizabeth had heard. Louella Belle tried to shame someone about their shape or implied a person would be better off if they just took her advice. Nothing that said "check here for a murder suspect."

Back at the station, Elizabeth called Skelly to see if he wanted to grab lunch in the diner. He promised to wash his hands well before joining her.

She smiled as she hung up. He had not come to town expecting to run for coroner, but thought the prior doctor who served as ME and coroner looked for easy reasons for causes of death.

Now he held the hospital appointment and elected position. Though most deaths he certified weren't crimes, the work kept him busy enough that he hadn't grown his internal medicine practice as much as he had planned.

Elizabeth deliberately arrived at the diner a few minutes before twelve, figuring someone might approach her about the murder. The weather had turned colder and the forecast was for freezing rain or sleet before the onslaught turned to snow. That seemed to have kept the diner's lunch crowd low.

Two booths down from Elizabeth sat two younger men she didn't know. Several booths in the other direction was Alice, the bookstore owner, who sat with Doris Minx. Alice waved without much apparent interest, and Doris turned to give Elizabeth a wide smile and wave before turning back to her lunch.

Nick negotiated around the five-foot Christmas tree that sat a few feet in front of the cash register as he deftly managed a large tray with three burger orders. He and Marti traded cooking duties. Neither of them especially liked to wait tables. A few customers might say neither was a standout cook, but overall Elizabeth thought the menu was better since they took over.

After he served the burgers Nick stopped at Elizabeth's booth. "Any news, Chief?"

She shook her head. "Not much. Still not sure who was last to see Louella Belle alive. You hear anything?"

"Nope. Funny how people aren't talking much about it. When Ben died, everyone said how sorry they were."

That made sense. The diner's prior owner might not have been Mr. Personality, but he was reasonably well liked. "Would you remember if Luella Belle often came in with a friend, or sat with the same people regularly?"

"Nope. I mean, I remember. No one sat with her. Can I get you something?"

"How about some decaf? I'll order when Skelly gets here."

As Nick turned toward the kitchen, Mayor Humphrey came in, shedding a huge red and green headscarf as she did so. She made for Elizabeth's booth, but correctly interpreted Elizabeth's lack of a smile as an indication that she was waiting for someone.

Humphrey paused at the booth. "I'm sure you would call me if you knew anything."

Elizabeth nodded. "We're making all the rounds."

The mayor leaned over. "I hear Jerry Pew is running a story with a list of suspects."

Elizabeth frowned. "That seems impossible, since I don't have any."

"Well now, maybe I didn't hear him right." She hesitated. "But I think I did."

"Did Jerry give you any names?"

Humphrey shook her head. "No. Again, maybe it's my ears, but I thought he implied he got information from you."

Elizabeth's eyebrows went up. "I'll have to go over my conversation with him."

"Oh, dear, don't say I told you what he said."

"No worries, Madam Mayor. I think it's just Jerry trying to pump you for information."

Humphrey shook her tightly permed head. "I should know better than to listen to him."

The diner door opened and a blast of air colder than it had been twenty minutes ago blew in with Skelly. He waved to Elizabeth and the mayor.

In a lower tone, Humphrey leaned closer to Elizabeth. "So, have a nice lunch." She waved at Skelly as she moved toward a booth at the far side of the diner.

"Will do." Elizabeth rolled her eyes at Skelly as he sat.

He shrugged out of a dark blue ski jacket and picked up a menu propped between the napkin holder and tall canister of sugar. "In cahoots with the mayor about something?"

"She told me Jerry Pew's pretending he knows something about who killed Louella Belle. I may have to put out a contract out on him."

Skelly pointed to Elizabeth's shoulder. "I see that cat of yours is shedding."

"Great." She glanced to her right and reached up to pluck two short, light brown cat hairs from her shoulder.

"Did you ever name that beast?"

Elizabeth shook her head. "I mentally think of her as Tortoise because she's a tortoise shell. Wish the woman who rented before me had taken her. Pretty mean to abandon her."

Skelly shrugged. "She knew your landlady had the place rented. Maybe better than the pound."

"Only by a hair." She grinned. "She hates being alone so much."

Skelly glanced out the diner's window at the sleet that had begun to turn the sidewalk to silver. "Better warm and dry than out in this."

"Wish it would fully convert to snow. At this rate we'll be called out to fender benders all afternoon."

Nick walked up with an open order book. "What'll it be, you two?"

Sometimes it irritated Elizabeth when people treated her and Skelly like a couple. Today she decided Nick would have said the same thing if she'd been sitting with Hammer or Calderone. "I'll have the Cobb salad, light on the ranch dressing, and a cup of tomato soup."

"Gimme a reuben, Nick. Heavy on the thousand island dressing. And you have any of Marti's famous apple cider pie?"

"Yep." He grinned momentarily. "But I made it this time. Helping with the baking because of the Louella Belle stuff."

"Is it safe to eat?" Skelly asked.

"Well..." Nick dragged out the word. "There might be a couple lumps of flour in the crust. But otherwise it's okay."

Elizabeth suppressed a smile as Skelly said, "I've eaten gravy with lumps of flour, so no problem in a piecrust."

Nick left as Elizabeth said, "You amaze me with your food choices. Why doesn't a doctor get the fresh chicken sandwich?"

"Because the doctor gives himself permission to eat what he wants a few times a week."

Nick returned with Elizabeth's decaf. "Sorry, forgot this." He looked at Skelly. "What do you want to drink?"

"Just water, thanks." As Nick walked away again, Skelly said, "Wish they hadn't stopped serving beer in the evenings. I liked grabbing one without sitting in the Weed 'n Feed or a bar."

Elizabeth grinned. "You don't like the aroma over there?"

Skelly shrugged. "Guess selling beer made it hard to get help here, since everyone would have to be over twenty-one."

A man's voice came from two booths behind them, speech mildly slurred. "Was cheaper here than the Weed 'n Feed, too."

Elizabeth turned. She didn't know the men, who were dressed more roughly than college students. Most of the students had gone home already, anyway. "Makes for a good family environment." She studied them for a few seconds before turning back to Skelly.

"Know them?" he asked, speaking softly.

"Nope. I think I've seen the heavier one with Finn Clancy at times."

"Without giving anything away, I've patched them both up, separately."

Elizabeth studied him. "Don't remember police reports with either of their pictures."

"Private fight, so to speak."

"Between the two of them?" Elizabeth asked.

"Don't think so. They both work evening shift at the meatpacking plant."

Skelly said nothing else as Nick placed a Reuben in front of him and the salad in front of Elizabeth. "Anything else, guys?"

"Got any more of that gingerbread Marti makes?" Elizabeth asked.

"Can't you smell it? She just took it out of the oven." He nodded at Skelly. "I'll bring your pie when I bring the chief her gingerbread."

"Bet the smell'll be out here in a couple of minutes," Elizabeth said.

Before she could ask Skelly the names of the two men, they spoke slightly louder, discussing the tip as they stood up to leave.

She put her fork in the salad. "When will you have the final autopsy report?"

"I'll get the preliminary bloodwork back this afternoon. Usually they try to culture a couple oddball things, and that takes a few days. Won't show anything."

The men nodded at Skelly as they walked by, and called for Nick as they got to the cash register.

They ate in silence until Elizabeth said, "I can't think of anyone who might've killed Louella Belle. I wouldn't be surprised if some people wished her dead."

"I didn't know her well. You think it could have been a robbery gone wrong?"

She shrugged. "No one recalls her showing a wad of bills when she paid for anything recently, and she wasn't known to carry a lot of cash or wear expensive jewelry."

Nick dropped off the desserts. "Thanks." Elizabeth turned her attention to the gingerbread as Skelly stabbed his apple cider pie with a fork.

She lifted her aromatic sweet to her mouth and took the first bite. "Mmm. Still warm."

Skelly put a huge forkful of pie in his mouth, then quickly grabbed his napkin and spit it out. "This tastes like…," he studied the barely chewed pie, "vinegar."

Elizabeth's own fork was still poised for a second bite of gingerbread. She placed it on the table. "Vinegar? Like it's spoiled?"

Skelly stuck a fork in the pie and held a piece toward her. "Don't eat it, just smell."

She sniffed. "It does smell like vinegar. Spoiled cider mixed with the apples, maybe."

Nick finished dealing with the two men who had just left the cash register, and he walked over. "Something wrong with the pie?"

Elizabeth thought Marti must have heard the question as she came through the swinging door from the kitchen.

"Well, Nick, maybe the cider was bad," Skelly said. "Did you buy it recently?"

Marti stood a few feet from them. "I just bought it at the store a few days ago. Hy-Vee buys it from the people who sell it at the farmers' market "

All eyes turned to Nick.

"Um, well, I don't think I used that jug."

Skelly's back had been to Marti, and he turned to face her. "You had an older batch of cider?"

She shook her head. "Just the one."

"See," Nick said, "this bottle was on the counter, near the refrigerator. It said apple cider."

Skelly started to laugh. Elizabeth didn't get what was funny.

Marti slapped her forehead. "Nick! That was apple cider vinegar!"

Nick's shoulders slumped. "I wondered how you got the pie to taste so good." He mumbled his way back to the kitchen.

When the laughter stopped and Elizabeth and Skelly assured Marti they didn't want a free lunch, Elizabeth turned to Skelly. "You could have at least accepted her offer to make you a pie for Christmas."

"Nah. I have one serving of apple cider pie a year. I'd just eat the whole pie. That could get rough on my stomach."

His comment reminded Elizabeth of the two men who had been sitting behind them. "What are their names? Those two guys who wished the Bully Pulpit still served beer."

Skelly said, "Because I told you they were patients, I won't give you their names. I'm sure you can find them pretty easily."

"I get it," Elizabeth said. But she didn't. However, she'd seen enough of the men to describe them to Hammer or one of the others. As long as the larger one, the one whose speech seemed slightly slurred, didn't drive, she didn't care about them. Unless they did laundry across the street.

CHAPTER TEN

BACK AT THE STATION AFTER lunch on Wednesday, Hammer had the phone at his ear, and she could hear Calderone and Mahan in the break room. Sounded as if they were discussing football, so she wouldn't head back there.

She had just settled at her desk to call Jerry Pew when Hammer knocked on her office's door jamb. "Either somebody's upping the ante or we have a new crackpot in town." He walked to her desk and handed Elizabeth a piece of lined white paper, which he had placed in a clear evidence bag. "Found this in the alley, near the corner of the building."

Elizabeth studied the note's block printing. "No one cares who killed Louella Bell. Stay away before somebody gets hurt."

Hammer shook his head slightly. "I read it, obviously. Seems if it were serious there'd be a more specific threat."

Elizabeth nodded. "Probably. Since no witness has been mentioned in the paper, and given where you found it, this seems to be directed at us." She handed him back the note. "I think we can take care of ourselves, but let the guys know about this."

He accepted it, but didn't turn to leave. "You want to keep the holiday schedule the same, or you want more of us on?"

She leaned back in her desk chair. "If Louella Belle were murdered today, so close to Christmas, I might rearrange. But we've done most of the interviews we can think of, and gathered any evidence from the scene."

Hammer nodded. "I saw you let Squeaky reopen the laundromat today."

Elizabeth grinned. "Did you see how he decorated it?"

"Nope."

"He has a Christmas tree in the window and most of the decorations are laundry detergent pods."

Hammer laughed as he turned toward the door. "Those'll be gone by Christmas Eve."

"Hey," Elizabeth called, "two guys were eating in the diner just now. Late twenties, probably. Skelly said they work at the packing plant, but didn't want to tell me their names."

Hammer's eyebrows shot up. "Why not?"

"Patients of his, sometimes. They could well be upstanding citizens, but they looked rough, and Skelly said they'd been in some fights. Sound familiar?"

"Nope. They still there when you left?"

"No. They could be nearby, or might have gone home or to work."

Hammer again turned toward the hallway. "I'll glance down the street a couple of times to see if I can see them hanging around."

Elizabeth thought about the two men as she placed her gun in the file cabinet, locked it, and returned to her desk to call Jerry Pew. He might know them, but she'd never ask.

She knew the newspaper phone number by heart. "Afternoon Jerry, hear you've stirred up some suspects in Louella Belle's death."

"Well now, Chief, I might be willing to compare notes before I run the story."

"Since I have none, that would be tough. You aren't holding onto information about a criminal act are you?" She wasn't about to use a term like obstructing justice. Jerry would get all 'protecting sources' on her.

"Now, if I knew something solid, I'd tell you so you could make an arrest."

Elizabeth took a sip of the cold coffee she'd left on her desk. "Thing is, if you have an inkling, I'm the one in the position to investigate. What did you hear?"

"Just rumors, mostly."

"Jerry, I'm serious. Do you know something I should know?" She emphasized the you and I.

Jerry muttered something Elizabeth couldn't hear.

"Anyone you suggest I talk to?"

"Nuthin' like that, Chief. Just rumors about people selling stuff in there."

"Are we talking Avon or Girl Scout cookies?" Elizabeth asked.

He grunted. "To be honest, I don't know. Just heard about money changing hands."

"Just money, or something with the money?"

Elizabeth could envision Jerry's gulp as he paused. "See, Chief, that's all I heard. I been goin' by there, in my car, now and again, to take a peek for myself."

"Okay, Jerry, here's the deal. You let us investigate. I have people keeping an eye on the laundromat."

"Did you..?"

She raised her voice. "When we know something, I mean know, not wonder about, I promise I will talk to you."

"Before the papers in Carlinville or Carbondale?"

Elizabeth almost laughed. Those towns were much bigger than Logland and had daily papers. "I'll talk to you first, but you know they might publish first. I can't wait two days before I talk to other news outlets."

"Yeah, I hear you. Well, I got that web page now. I don't put the whole articles on there, but if I get the story first I can put it on the web."

Elizabeth tried to keep impatience out of her voice. "Fine. Now, what do you actually know?"

"You heard Finn Clancy is in there a lot?"

"Later in the evening. Is it every day, Jerry?"

"Course, I only been paying attention the last few days. And Squeaky only reopened today."

Elizabeth stifled a curse. "So, Jerry, guess we found out the same stuff. If you let people think you know secrets, you could put a bulls-eye on your back. Leave the investigating to us, and I'll tell you what we find when it can be public."

"How about off the record sometimes, Chief?"

"We'll see. Don't slide on the ice." She hung up.

Male voices burst into laughter outside her door. Hammer walked into her office, followed by Calderone and Mahan.

Elizabeth stared at the men. She appreciated all of them, and like most of the force, they worked hard. But she wanted at least one of them to retire so she could hire younger people, officers who could deal more easily with the college students. And she needed at least one more woman in the ranks.

"Okay, guys. Did you know how little Jerry knew?"

Calderone sat on one corner of her desk, while Hammer and Mahan stayed in the doorway. Calderone grinned. "You gotta figure Jerry can't keep his trap shut, whether he knows anything or not. Mahan here thought you'd tear him a new one."

Mahan straightened to his full five-feet eight. "Now, I don't talk like that to the Chief."

Elizabeth raised her eyebrows at him. "You forgot I worked in Chicago for five years?"

"No, ma'am. But I figure you're here now, and you don't talk like some big city cops."

"Good observation. Who checked out Squeaky's change machine?"

They sobered. "I did," Hammer said. "And then I asked Mahan to take a look because I thought the scratches around the lock could mean somebody was trying to jimmy it."

Elizabeth looked at Mahan.

"I thought so, too," he said. "Maybe somebody using a tiny flat screwdriver. You know, trying to work the lock but slipping with the tool now and then. But the lock doesn't look damaged."

"Prints?" she asked.

"Took a few from there three nights ago," Calderone said. "Hadn't made the ones from the change machine a high priority request with AFIS, but I'm about to bug them about all the prints."

Elizabeth pointed to the several chairs scattered near her desk. "Pull up a seat." As they did, she added, "Skelly said Louella Belle could have hit her head on the lip of the laundry tub in the back corner. Injured her neck pretty badly, maybe made her pass out."

They nodded in tandem. "Saw his draft report," Calderone said.

"So, that's pretty far from the front of the store, where the bill changer is. But she could have seen something odd in the front, gotten scared, and run toward the back if she couldn't get out the front door to the street."

"You think someone killed her because she saw them trying to take a bunch of quarters?" Mahan asked.

"No, but someone could have run after her to talk, grabbed her arm and she fell. I figure the odds of her murder being planned are pretty slim."

"You didn't have to take home nutrition from her in high school," Hammer said.

"Wasn't she after your time?" Elizabeth asked.

"Ouch," Calderone said.

Hammer half smiled. "My youngest brother had her. And my oldest sister's children. The kids mostly ignored her, but when parents went in for parent-teacher conferences, she lectured them on what they fed their kids."

Mahan frowned. "She told my next-door neighbor that her daughter was going to be a fat lady in the circus if she didn't quit feeding the kid junk food."

"Good God," Elizabeth said.

Mahan nodded. "Principal made her write a letter of apology. Never figured out why she didn't get fired."

"Spend a lot of time thinking about it?" Calderone asked.

"Shut up," Mahan said, but good naturedly.

"How long has she been retired?" Elizabeth asked.

Calderone pulled a notebook from his shirt pocket. "Six-and-a-half years ago. Far as anyone knows, she didn't take a job after she retired."

Elizabeth leaned back in her desk chair. "That means she was past seventy when she stopped working. She must have liked her job."

Calderone shrugged. "She doesn't have family or, as far as I can tell, friends. Maybe she didn't know what to do without a job."

"I wonder how she did spend her days?" Elizabeth mused.

Mahan said, "She did a couple talks about healthy eating at the library, but after a couple of sessions, no one went back. She did volunteer at the summer lunch program every year, where kids can eat at the rec center for free."

Elizabeth nodded. "I know the program, but I only visited twice. Don't think I saw her."

"Sometimes she served food, but mostly they had her making calls to get food donations from local businesses and food banks and stuff. Lady who runs the program said she was pretty good at that."

"Glad to hear it," Elizabeth said, "first positive thing I've heard about her. But the program doesn't run during other vacations, does it?"

All three men said, no, and Calderone added, "She used to volunteer at the food bank, but she badgered them about using more organic food. They finally said she could only come if she quit lecturing people, so she stopped coming."

Elizabeth shook her head. "Sounds more like her." She looked at each man in turn. "So, we still know next to nothing? Did she even do her laundry there?"

"Nope," Hammer said. "She had a nice washer and dryer at her place. Small house, but everything ship-shape when we checked it the day after she was killed."

Elizabeth focused on Calderone. "When did you say you'd get any fingerprint matches?"

He stood. "Could have some in my email now."

The phone ringing in the bullpen reminded Elizabeth it had been quiet for the last hour. "No calls?"

Hammer glanced back at her as he hurried out the door. "Guess everyone's in for the storm."

CHAPTER ELEVEN

ELIZABETH HEADED TO THE Dollar General once Calderone said he hadn't gotten any fingerprint info and would follow up on the request. The older Crown Vic she drove while on duty would have been mothballed in a larger town, but it had fewer than 30,000 miles on it. With its large engine, the car did not do well on the ice. Or it slid well, if that was your perspective.

The store had few customers. Elizabeth stomped on the black mat to rid her boots of snow and ice melt pellets.

Blake Wessley greeted her politely, but with a sour expression. She judged he had lost several pounds, because his square-jawed face appeared thinner, giving him a haggard expression. Or maybe he slept less since he had to work. He still managed to look fastidious, in pressed blue jeans and a collared St. Louis Cardinals shirt.

Wessley stopped restocking the Christmas candy shelf. "My manager said you would stop by. I didn't know the woman who died. I mean, I read the story about her death."

"I know you didn't go to high school here. I'm more interested in regular goings-on in the laundromat. Did you ever see one customer act hostile to another? Anything like that?"

"No. I try to go in the daytime when I can. Mostly men who work at the meat-packing plant go in the evening. Few guys from Sweathog, but all the women and most of the students do laundry during the day."

Elizabeth nodded. "I've heard older folks go mostly in the daytime, too. Someone else implied it was a tougher crowd after dark."

Wessley shrugged. "I've talked to a few of them. Not bad guys, just...rough around the edges, maybe." He pulled a bunch of foil-wrapped marshmallow Santas from a box and began placing them on a lower shelf.

Elizabeth studied his profile, "How about Finn Clancy?"

Wessley half-turned. "He's a lazy grifter, but I've never seen him bother anyone."

"Did you hear someone stole his bike?"

Wessley's laugh was harsh. "Too bad he didn't seem the type to have insurance. He could use a new one."

"Rusty. I saw it once." She took a card from the pocket of her jacket. "You might overhear conversations in here. Don't get involved in anything, but if you learn something useful, call me."

Wessley accepted the card, slowly. "President Dodd said you recommended not expelling us."

"I know you faced some charges for the fireworks and a couple other things. Figured that could be enough punishment."

He pocketed the card. "My dad got me a good lawyer. I'm on probation for a year, and got a fine and other stuff." He bent down to the cardboard box of candy again. "If I hear anything, I'll call you."

As she left the store, Elizabeth pulled her collar up so the stiff breeze didn't waft down her neck. She felt as if she was spinning her wheels on more than ice.

ELIZABETH HADN'T EXPECTED to see any other former frat brothers, but Monty came in that afternoon as she stood at Hammer's desk signing time sheets. Unlike the pasty-skinned, active alcoholic who weaved when he walked, a healthy man of nineteen stood before her.

"Hello, Chief Friedman. Did you recognize me?" He extended a hand across the counter.

"She took it. You look terrific, Monty. I like the maroon sweater."

From his desk chair, Hammer said, "You do look good. Congratulations."

Final Cycle

He sombered. "It's always one day at a time, but today I'm good. Thanks."

"Can we help you with anything?" Elizabeth asked.

He had held one hand at this side, and now used it to place a large box of Whitman Sampler candies on the counter. "Merry Christmas." He looked past Elizabeth to Hammer. "To all of you guys. You treated me decent, and I probably don't remember much of anything."

Elizabeth smiled. "I'm glad you're home for the holidays." She pulled the box of candy to her and ran a finger along the protective cellophane to open the box.

"If I can make things work at home, I'll stay and go back to school in January."

Elizabeth remembered that Monty's parents had seemed very rigid. Rigid and unhappy that a third-generation Sweathog attendee had been a full-blown drunk. "They support you not drinking, though, right?"

"Oh, yeah." He waved as Elizabeth pushed the now-open candy box to him. "Swore off chocolate, too."

"Jeez," Hammer said. "I'd never make it through Christmas without chocolate."

Sensing he wanted to leave, Elizabeth said, "Thanks for the candy, Monty."

He threw a dark green, long scarf around one shoulder, so it hugged his neck more. "Least I can do." He turned and went back to the biting cold and snow."

Elizabeth turned to Hammer. "Made my day."

Hammer nodded. Before he could comment, Calderone called from the hall. "Chief, you got a call."

Elizabeth walked back to her office, glanced at the blinking light on the station's outdated phone, and pushed it. "Chief Friedman here."

"Elizabeth? It's Edna."

Elizabeth sat up straighter. Her landlord had never called her at work. "Everything okay, Edna?"

"You need to come home to look for your cat."

"Excuse me?"

"Someone threw a brick through your kitchen window. So hard it shattered. That cat of yours squeezed out the opening."

CHAPTER TWELVE

ELIZABETH STOOD AS SHE spoke and walked to her locked file cabinet to retrieve her gun. "I'm on my way. I'll bring someone with me to check around. Please lock yourself in your apartment."

"Oh, I did as soon as I went outside and saw it. Your cat ran across the street, into the yard with all the lawn ornaments."

Elizabeth hung up and yelled, "Calderone. You're with me."

She walked into the bullpen as Calderone stood to shrug into his jacket. "What's up, Chief?"

"Somebody threw a brick through my apartment window and my cat got out."

Simultaneously, Hammer said, "You should take Mahan, too," and Mahan said, "You have a cat?"

"I'd rather have two of you here in case we get more calls. Don't think the person hung around. Let the guys on patrol know." She strode toward the door. "Calderone, you're driving."

He jiggled his keys as he followed her out. "Watch your step."

Elizabeth almost skidded on a fresh sheen of ice on the sidewalk. "Jeez." She turned toward the station's large window and pointed down to the sidewalk as she walked.

Inside, Hammer nodded to her.

Elizabeth buckled her seatbelt and Calderone turned on his lights and siren. "I didn't hear a 9-1-1 call come in."

"My landlord, Edna, called me directly. I'll remind her to use 9-1-1 in the future."

They didn't speak as Calderone drove the ten blocks to Elizabeth's apartment in Edna Brown's large Victorian house. They were within a few yards of the house when a streak of brown tore across the street. Calderone braked and they skidded to a stop, but not before Elizabeth heard a shriek from her cat.

"Damn, Chief, I'm sorry if I…"

"Don't worry about it. She kept running." Her heart hammered as she pushed the cat from her mind and climbed out of the car, gun drawn. She surveyed the lawn as she walked across the grass toward the porch. Elizabeth had a private side entry, with external stairs leading up to it, but wanted to talk to Edna first.

The bolt on the front door slid open as Elizabeth and Calderone climbed the slippery front porch steps.

Edna, sporting a holiday-themed red sweatshirt with a small Christmas tree surrounded by tame wildlife, had her mouth in a wide O. "Goodness, you didn't need to use the siren."

Elizabeth forced a smile. "Thought we'd scare away any bad guys if they were still hanging around."

"Can we get upstairs from the inside?" Calderone asked.

With her eye on Elizabeth's gun as she holstered it, Edna said, "Yes, Tony, but you wipe your boots really well." She pointed toward her kitchen, in the back of the first floor.

"Steps are behind the fridge," Elizabeth said. She focused on Edna. "Are you all right? Do you want to call your son?"

"No! He'd be all bent out of shape. I'm fine."

Elizabeth gestured to Edna's sofa and sat across from it in a pale blue, stuffed chair. "What else can you tell us?"

"Nothing, I don't think. I didn't go up there. I have a stiff broom you can use to sweep up the glass.

"Just a second." Elizabeth walked to the foot of the steps that led upstairs. "Calderone. All clear up there?"

"Think so. I'll check the other rooms if you don't mind."

"Sure." *Good thing I made my bed and put yesterday's clothes in the hamper.*

She walked back to Edna. "Okay, if you're all right, I'm going outside to see if I can see my cat." She walked onto the front porch and scanned the snowy yard.

Something brown and the size of a large ham crawled out from under an evergreen bush. "Oh, baby, you're hurt." She almost skidded down the steps, but when she bent over to pick up the cat, it meowed plaintively.

Edna called from the porch. "Let me get a box. Easier to carry her if she's hurt."

Calderone called from the top of the external staircase on the side of the house. "Looks okay except for the bricks...No! Did I hit it?"

Tears stung Elizabeth's eyes, but she kept her voice steady. "She's going to be okay. And no, you didn't hit her. She ran in front of our car."

"Tony, dear. Come get this box. It's too cold for me out there."

Calderone had been en route from the side staircase to where Elizabeth knelt, but he detoured and grabbed the low-sided box and brought it to Elizabeth.

The cat lay on its side, breathing more heavily than usual.

"How should we lift her?" Calderone asked.

As Elizabeth started to suggest that he hold the box and she try to slide the cat into it, Skelly's green Camry pulled to the curb. He hurried to them, almost slipping on the thin sheen of ice on the sidewalk.

"Good God, Elizabeth." He knelt next to the cat and touched her head lightly. "Someone hit her?"

"I did," Calderone said.

"No," Elizabeth insisted. "She dashed in front of the patrol car."

Snow soaked his hospital scrubs as Skelly continued to kneel. He ran a hand down the cat's coat, not pressing hard. "She doesn't look misshapen. I bet she has a bruised pelvis not a broken one. Better that than being hit in the mid-section."

Elizabeth felt her eyes start to tear again. "You think so?"

Skelly glanced at her and back to the cat. "Let me take her to the vet. If he gives her the okay I'll take her back to the hospital with me so she can't get out again. I bet she'll be fine."

Elizabeth did her best to sound practical. "Okay, help me get her in this box."

Calderone knelt to steady the box as Elizabeth put a hand under and just below the cat's head, and Skelly did the same at her pelvis. The cat meowed in slight protest, but didn't try to get away or bite.

The three stood together. Skelly held the box carefully and moved toward his car. "I'll call you."

Elizabeth looked back to Calderone. "I paid too much attention to my cat. Sorry. Tell me what you found."

Calderone turned toward the external stairs and she followed him. "If itta been my dog, I'd be blubbering like a kid."

"Didn't know you had a dog."

He grinned. "A mutt. My ex-wife and I share it."

Now and then Elizabeth realized how little she knew about her officers' lives. They'd had a welcome picnic for her when she arrived, and she'd gone to one wedding, but not anything less formal, like kids' birthday parties. It was hard enough to be the only woman in a department, and she didn't want to socialize a lot outside of work.

"Joint custody. Very amicable of you. What did you find besides the brick, or whatever it was, and a bunch of glass?"

"It's two bricks tied together with some kind of heavy twine. Guess that's why it made such a big hole. Paper under the twine, around the bricks, is probably some kind of note."

They entered Elizabeth's kitchen and looked at the smattering of glass all over the floor. The bricks rested next to the baseboard in front of the refrigerator. "Could be worse, I guess," Elizabeth said.

Calderone's radio buzzed and he clicked it. "Hey, we're good over here."

Hammer's voice came through. "Seemed calm enough that Mahan's bringing you the small crime scene kit. Then he'll swing back."

Calderone winked at Elizabeth. "I hit the chief's cat."

"What the f…?!"

Elizabeth raised her voice. "No, he didn't. She ran in front of the car as we pulled up. Skelly came by and got her. He doesn't think anything's broken."

Hammer picked up on her light tone. "Better hope not. That would be a hell of a demerit on your next performance report, Calderone."

He grimaced, but his eyes crinkled. "I'm gonna sweep up the glass all over the place, check out the bricks. Some kind of note wrapped around them. Be back after that."

Hammer signed off, and Elizabeth said, "Edna says she has a stiff broom. Mine's softer. I'll go reassure her and come back with the broom."

Elizabeth went down the inside staircase, got the broom, and came back as Mahan arrived with the forensic kit. "Sorry about your window, Chief. And the cat."

"The person had to know I wouldn't be home, so I guess this is as destructive as he plans to get."

"Or she," both men said.

Elizabeth glanced at her window. "I don't mean to sound sexist, but that throw, from the ground up, took a lot more muscle than most women have."

Mahan grinned. "I'm damn glad she said that."

"All right, you two. I'll clean up here if you want to ask a couple neighbors if they saw anything."

Mahan nodded. "Calderone can do that. I'll get a piece of Plexiglas at the hardware store. You got a tape measure?"

"That's above and beyond," Elizabeth said.

"Nah. I do it now and again. Better than a board until Edna gets a glass guy to fix it."

Calderone looked up from where he'd been kneeling next to the bricks, and grinned. "He mostly does it for old people."

"Two demerits," Elizabeth said.

AFTER HAMMER CAREFULLY UNTIED the note, Elizabeth, he, and Calderone stood in the station's conference room to read it together. "Who spells that badly?" Elizabeth asked.

"I tole you to back off. Your place will be more than chile if you don't leave Louella Bell's murder alone."

"Misspells Louella Belle's name the same as the note a couple days ago. And *chile* instead of *chilly*," Hammer said.

"Probably deliberate," Elizabeth said, "so we think the person isn't well-educated."

Calderone snorted. "Could be well educated, but throwing a brick through the police chief's window isn't smart."

"And no prints," Elizabeth murmured. "We're no further ahead than we were a couple of hours ago."

"In some ways we are," Calderone said. "We know someone, probably local, is paying attention to the investigation."

Hammer turned toward the door, but stopped. "How's your cat?"

Elizabeth raised her eyebrows at him. "Does Skelly pay you for tipoffs?"

Hammer sighed. "He buys lots of Girl Scout cookies from my oldest daughter. So when he asked me to let him know if you were hurt or anything…" His voice trailed off.

"Is that a bribe, Calderone?" she asked, careful not to smile.

"I think it's gotta be money to be a bribe," Calderone threw in.

"Technically, anything of value," Hammer began. He stopped when Elizabeth pointed to the door to the hallway with her thumb.

"Go away."

Calderone had brought in two large plastic bags, each with a sliding closure. "I'll put these in evidence, even though they didn't have prints." He gloved each hand and reached for the first brick.

Elizabeth turned toward the hallway, planning to head to her office. "I doubt it'll help, but show the note to the others to see if the penmanship looks familiar."

Her phone rang and Elizabeth glanced at the caller ID. "Good, Skelly. Talk to you in a minute, Calderone."

"After all you've put her through, you really should name your cat," Skelly said.

"I'll take it under advisement. How is she?"

"Only one vet at Happy Animal Care today, so they're swamped. I x-rayed her here. Nothing broken. Vet's office gave me a mild sedative for her and she's sleeping."

"I can't thank you enough."

"You're staying in town. Have Christmas Eve dinner with me."

Elizabeth hesitated for a second. He'd just more or less rescued her cat. She couldn't say no. "Okay, come up with some names."

"Lucky will be first on that list."

CHAPTER THIRTEEN

ELIZABETH'S CELL RANG AT three o'clock Wednesday afternoon. She groaned when she saw Wally Kermit's name. He would never take the hint to call the station.

"Chief, I think I found that bike."

Elizabeth closed her desk drawer and stood. She thought Wally sounded nervous. "Great. Where was it?"

"You know that dumpster behind Alice's bookstore?"

Exasperation flooded Elizabeth. "Kind of far from campus, Wally."

"Well, yeah, but like I told you, I had a couple days off." When Elizabeth said nothing for a second, he added, "Kinda cold out here."

"Sorry, didn't realize you were outside. Is the bookstore open?"

"I think she's open until six, seeing's how it's close to Christmas."

"Head inside. One of us will meet you there." Elizabeth hung up, frustrated. She doubted Wally had been able to keep his hands off the bicycle.

"Hammer! Who's around?"

"Just me," he called. "Fender bender right outside the college entrance. Mahan's there. Calderone's at the hardware store trying to figure out if they sell the color brick that sailed through your window."

Elizabeth took her coat from a hook on the back of her office door and walked the short distance to the bullpen to stand next to Hammer's desk. "Wally may have found the bike. I'll head down to the dumpster behind the bookstore to see if it's Finn Clancy's rusty set of wheels."

Hammer stood. "It's a mess out there. I'll go."

"Only witches melt in the rain."

Hammer frowned. "I get you can tolerate the snow."

She grinned at him. "Besides, Grayson will be in soon for his shift. I need you to be sure he's alert."

Hammer half-snorted. "He's always wide awake early in his shift."

Elizabeth strode toward the door. "I have my radio, in case we lose cell service."

Heavy snow had begun falling an hour earlier, so her boots crunched on the sidewalk instead of slipped. She started her car, turned the defroster on high, and muttered, "We gotta get some kind of carport built behind the station."

She groped under her seat for the long scraper with a brush on one end. Maybe she could add a carport to her next budget request. *Third time's the charm*. Dingle might feel guilty enough about Louella Belle not to fight her about it at a City Council meeting.

She finished scraping the windshield and side windows, and blessed the rear defroster for saving her the added time in the cold. She climbed in the warming car and pulled into traffic. Driving was easier now because snow covered the ice and a lot of people had headed home early.

Alice's bookstore was a popular place at Christmastime. Much of the year her best customers were college students trading in books. She paid them more than the college book exchange. At Halloween and Christmas, she kept a hectic pace, though Halloween was more for novelty items than books.

Elizabeth glanced at the decorated windows on each side of the door. A huge gingerbread house looked as if it had been built by different people, some of them surely visually impaired. She entered the store and stomped her feet on the large black mat.

Alice's voice came from an aisle or two away. "Afternoon, Elizabeth. Wally's in the restroom."

Elizabeth brushed snow from her coat onto the mat. "Thanks. Sorry to trouble you."

Final Cycle

"Not at all. He said we weren't in any danger. I'm glad if you found something that will help you solve Louella Belle's murder."

Danger, Elizabeth thought. Just like Wally to be dramatic.

Alice came into view, wearing a Mrs. Santa outfit and horizontally striped tights, kind of like Elf in the holiday movie. Her long, white hair hung in a braid that poked out of the Mrs. Santa hat. "When you go outside, you can use my rear door rather than drive around. It's just a few feet from the dumpster."

"Thanks. By any chance do you know when the bike appeared back there?"

"I took trash out just before I opened at ten this morning. I'm sure I would have noticed it. When Wally showed it to me, you could see one of the tires kind of sticks out from behind the trash thingy."

Wally's voice drifted toward them. "Hey, Chief."

Elizabeth glanced at him and away. Apparently he'd been in a hurry, because his zipper was halfway down. "Great job, Wally, thanks."

With a puffed out chest, he gestured that she should follow him to the exit that led to the alley. "I scouted the area. Didn't see anyone in the alley."

Alice hid a smile as she met Elizabeth's gaze. The front door opened and she hurried toward a customer who seemed to be holding a long list of things to buy.

"So, Wally, did the bike have a lot of snow on it when you found it?"

"Inch or so on the seat, not so much on the handlebars. They're kind of angled, you know?"

"Right. I remember it sort of looked like a racing bike."

"Maybe ten years ago," Wally said.

Elizabeth smiled. "I didn't pay a lot of attention to it when I saw it in the alley the night Louella Belle was killed, but it appeared to have lived a couple of lives."

They entered Alice's storage room and Wally rushed to the exit door. He held it so Elizabeth could precede him into the alley.

She placed her flat hat on her head again and followed him into the snow, which wasn't falling as hard as it had been a few minutes ago. Sure enough, the bike leaned against the dumpster. The front headlight dangled. She didn't remember that from the other night. But even in the deepening twilight, she felt certain it was the same crummy, rusty bike.

No tracks in the snow. She'd been wrong; Wally hadn't touched it. "What made you look back here?"

He nodded toward one of the electric blue Sweathog security cars. He had parked it behind a business two doors down, so Elizabeth hadn't noticed it.

"I been driving through the alleys a couple times a day. Almost as many alley miles as street miles in this town."

"Was this your first pass through here today?"

He nodded. "Yep. Alice told me she didn't see it this morning, but she hasn't been out here since maybe nine-thirty or ten."

Elizabeth studied the bike. "Big gap in time. No tracks in the snow, though, so must have been here at least a couple hours."

"Handlebars don't look icy," Wally said. "Maybe someone left it here after the sleet stopped."

Elizabeth thought she should give the man more credit, powdered donuts aside. "Good observation. Come on, let's go back inside."

Wally seemed reluctant to leave the alley, even though snow had picked up again. "Hope no one takes it."

Elizabeth nodded at the bike. "It lists. I bet the tires are flat."

"Good eye, Chief."

Inside again, Elizabeth pulled her phone from her jacket pocket and nodded to Wally. "I'll get Hammer to send someone down for the bike."

He brushed snow from his security uniform jacket. "Yeah, won't fit in the Sweathog car's trunk."

Elizabeth listened to the phone ring at the station. "We'll use a...hey, Hammer. It is Finn Clancy's bike."

She listened as he said he'd try to get a tow truck, but it could take a while. "Lots of fender benders, Chief. Because of the ice under the snow."

Final Cycle

She didn't like using anything other than a flatbed tow truck, but Hammer had a point. "I agree. The crown vic's trunk is huge. Grayson in yet?"

"Yep. He's in the locker room."

"Okay, send him down with a bunch of latex gloves. They'll probably freeze and rip while we load the thing."

"I got a bunch in my glove box," Wally said.

Elizabeth shook her head as she hung up. "It's great that you found it, but it's part of a murder investigation. I need to make sure we keep track of it now."

He looked disappointed "Sure, chain of evidence and all that."

She added, "I can't thank you enough."

Alice stuck her head in the storage room. "You two can come into the main store. Was it the bike you wanted?"

"I think so." Elizabeth said. "You look ready for the holiday."

Wally trailed the two women as they talked.

"Thank you. I'm feeling better. Took me a while to get over the shock of Ben's death."

"True for a lot of people," Elizabeth said. "I know you didn't see anyone put the bike back there, but it seems it had to be someone local. Did you notice anyone in the store or nearby who isn't usually in this part of town?"

They had reached the front counter, and Alice walked behind it to the cash register. Alice shook her head, slowly. "Of course, people we don't often see have been in the bookstore, the dollar store, other shops. Christmas shopping. But no one stands out."

"Hardware store around the corner's busy," Wally said. "Selling trees and decorations and stuff."

"True," Alice said. "The people I've seen who aren't here often are the usual holiday shoppers."

Wally leaned on the counter, facing Alice more directly. "Anybody look shifty?"

Alice's laugh was light and high. "Wally! You watch too much TV."

Elizabeth hid a smile. "It's good to pay attention to different behaviors, but our bike person probably stayed out of view."

Red and blue lights from outside bounced on the bookstore windows, announcing Grayson.

Alice frowned and gestured to the window. "Elizabeth, do tell him to turn those off. People will stay away."

"Will do, Alice. Thanks for the warmth." Elizabeth walked to the front door, Wally trailing behind her.

She put her cap on as she walked outside, and made a rolling gesture with her fist and arm, letting Grayson know she wanted to talk to him.

He rolled his driver's window partway down. "Out back, Chief?"

"Yes. But turn off your lights. Alice is afraid you'll scare away customers."

"Yes ma'am." He grinned. "See you in the alley."

As he pulled away, Elizabeth turned to Wally, and almost wanted to grit her teeth as she said, "Again, thanks. I usually bring in some cookies and such Christmas Eve. Feel free to come by the station in the afternoon for a few minutes."

CHAPTER FOURTEEN

WITH THE BIKE STOWED in the closet-sized property room about four o'clock, Elizabeth called Finn Clancy from her office.

He spoke as soon as he picked up the phone. "Hey, Chief. When can I come get my ride?"

She hated caller ID sometimes, but was more irritated that he knew it had been found. Probably lots of people had noticed the squad car and the bike she and Grayson loaded into her trunk. "I'm sorry, Mr. Clancy. We'll need to keep it for possible use at a trial, maybe…"

Clancy's curses weren't unique, but they were clear. "I need that bike!"

"I know you want us to catch Louella Belle's killer."

Clancy said nothing.

"I do want to be sure of something, Mr. Clancy. You probably heard we found it behind the dumpster in back of the bookstore. I saw it behind Gene's tattoo place. That's not too far from where Louella Belle was killed. Are you sure you left the bike in the rack by Doris Minx's cookie place?"

"Do you know where you parked that big boat police car you drive?"

"Most days. I'm not insulting your intelligence, just making sure we know the sequence of events."

"Yeah, all right. But I need that bike back now, not later."

"Let me think for a minute," Elizabeth said. When Clancy said nothing, she added, "Call me in the morning." She hung up without saying goodbye.

If Mahan hadn't checked at the Weed 'n Feed to be sure Clancy had been in there at the time they thought Louella Belle had been murdered, he'd be her prime suspect. Finn Clancy was a lazy, rude, crude man. But he didn't own a car, and in Logland a bike would get him most places he needed to go.

She stood from her desk and made for the bullpen. Hammer had the phone angled on his shoulder and chin, pen in hand, as he made notes. He rolled his eyes at her. Elizabeth figured someone had a snow-clearing request.

He hung up. "They think we'll call the plows to tell them to head to their street."

Elizabeth nodded. "And you explained they do most-traveled streets first, of course."

"I did. What's up?"

"Would you call the hardware store to see what's the best deal they can give us on a cheap men's bike?"

"For Clancy?"

"Yeah. I thought I could ask a bunch of people to kick in five bucks. We'll have to hold onto his for probably months."

Hammer snorted. "It'll have rusted through before then."

"I can pony up for all of it, I just don't want him thinking it all comes from me."

He nodded and reached into his hip pocket.

Elizabeth shook her head and grinned. "Save it for your kids. I think I might call Dingle."

Hammer laughed. "He can pass the hat at city hall."

She'd been at her desk less than five minutes when Calderone stuck his head in her office. "Your bricks aren't sold at the hardware store. But fingerprint results from the laundromat came in."

She gestured to a chair. "What does it tell us?"

"Probably nothing about Louella Belle's killer. Only eight people in the system. Those two people from the senior apartments. Theirs were on file because they used to teach. Squeaky's." He looked up from his notes. "Did you know he had a DUI up in Springfield fifteen years ago?"

"No. Just the one?"

"Yeah. We kind of keep an eye on him, since he weaves when he walks sometimes. Never saw him drive impaired."

"Guess he learned his lesson. Who else?"

"Your favorite frat guy, Blake Wessley."

"From any relevant machines?" she asked.

"Couple washers, different dryer. Finn Clancy's. I knew he'd be in the system." He looked up from his list. "I arrested him for a couple of bar fights, but he didn't start them."

"Were his prints on Louella Belle's dryer?"

"That's the kicker," Calderone said. "I got a couple from there, but they turned out to be Marti's. Hers went in the system as elimination prints when Ben died."

"So, we knew she touched the dryer."

"Yeah, but I got several prints there. Because they were only hers, it means someone wiped it down after they put Louella Belle in there."

"Huh." Elizabeth leaned back in her chair. "Probably a very quick crime. Seems like Blake Wessley, Stanley, and Grace were there within a few minutes of each other. Herbie and Just Juice were in there around the same time. Marti found her about six. But the person knew to avoid leaving prints."

Calderone frowned. "Yeah, but...could have been before five. Remember, Marti and Nick said Louella Belle left the diner about two o'clock. The little window in the dryer showed only the checkered tablecloth when Marti got there. Someone could have put her in there earlier and covered the little window."

"You're right. I hope Skelly can give us a more precise window."

"So to speak." He grinned and regarded his notes again. "Lots of prints around the change machine lock."

"Whose?"

"I believe they're called Just Juice and Herbie Hiccup."

Elizabeth pointed her index finger at Calderone. "Get them back here."

CALDERONE STUCK HIS HEAD IN Elizabeth's office. "I called places to chow down. Found Herbie and Just Juice at the

Weed 'n Feed. I told them to stop drinking for an hour, except for coffee, and come on over."

"You sure they weren't really wasted?"

Calderone shook his head. "You know the manager, Harvey Hunter, right?"

Elizabeth nodded.

"He said they only got there forty-five minutes ago."

Elizabeth glanced at the wall clock. "It's four-thirty, your shift ended an hour ago. Go home."

"You sure?"

"Hammer'll be here another hour, and Grayson's around."

"Great. I'll finish my shopping."

Elizabeth liked working with Calderone. Mature but not old-fashioned, and he had a good sense of humor. For a minute she felt lonely. She planned to cover Christmas Day, so wasn't going to visit family in Chicago. Just her and…

"Damn! The cat." She dialed Skelly's cell. "How's my girl?"

"Hello, Elizabeth. I'm fine, too."

She heard the humor in his voice. "Sorry. It's been so hectic I actually forgot about both of you for a couple hours."

"She's more awake. I think the sedative calmed her tense muscles. Vet also gave me two doses of oral pain meds. I'll dose her again before I bring her to you."

"Oh, I should do it. She bites when I try to give her pills."

"Liquid. I'll put the little syringe under her tongue and squirt."

"Great. So, I have what I hope is a short interview in the station in a few minutes, then I could get her from you."

"I have a couple errands. I put her in a box with one of those white hospital blankets. She'll be okay in the car while I grab a couple groceries. Meet you at the diner?"

"Uh, okay, but she may pee on your blanket."

"Nope. I keep cat litter in the closet here."

"You bring cats to work often?"

Skelly chuckled. "Good to clean up spills. We won't say of what."

"Ugh. I'll call your cell when I leave my office."

She hung up and walked to Hammer's desk. "Calderone tell you the two guys are coming by?"

"Yep. I had to look up their real names."

Elizabeth smiled. "Remind me."

" Erasmus Jenson and Herbert Gibson," he said.

"Okay. I'm going to make some official notes about what I heard today. Call me when they get here. I'll meet them in the conference room."

Elizabeth grabbed coffee from the break room and turned on her computer. She kept her handwritten notes, of course, but after a couple weeks they became harder to decipher.

When she started to write about the brick through her window, she paused. She didn't often discuss where she lived, and her address had never been in the paper. How had the brick tosser known her address?

Elizabeth had asked Edna not to broadcast who her tenant was, but she could have mentioned it in the grocery store or hair salon. In a small town, residents expected to know where everyone lived. Mentioning Elizabeth's address would not even have seemed like gossip to most people. The glass breaker probably did not have to look too hard to find her home.

She had just finished detailing about the brick thrown through her apartment window when her phone buzzed. "Yes?"

Hammer said, "Hey, Chief. The guys just came in. I'll take them back to the conference room."

She spoke quietly. "I'm going to let them simmer for a couple of minutes."

"Sounds like a plan." Hammer hung up.

She sent the day's notes to the printer, stood to stretch, and removed the paper from her printer to place in a file folder. She decided that was long enough to keep Herbie Hiccup and Just Juice on pins and needles.

Elizabeth walked down the hall to the conference room. "Mr. Gibson, Mr. Jenson. Thanks for coming back in." She sat opposite them at the table.

If they had been standing, Elizabeth could envision them shuffling their feet. Instead, they shifted in their respective chairs and met her eyes for only a second.

Herbie said, "Did you forget to ask us something?"

"We want to help," Just Juice added.

"That's terrific. Let's start with the laundromat's change machine."

"Uh, sure," Herbie said.

When Just Juice said nothing, Elizabeth asked, "Why do you think your fingerprints were all over that machine, especially around the lock?"

Herbie answered so fast Elizabeth thought they had rehearsed the response. "See, one day, it took our five dollar bill but didn't give us change."

Just Juice nodded very fast, which exercised his double chin.

"So, what made the little scratches?" Elizabeth asked.

Herbie said, "My pen."

Just Juice said, "My nail clipper."

Herbie's eyes widened and came back to normal size. Just Juice reddened.

"Ah," Elizabeth frowned. "I take it you tried more than a couple of times."

"It was five bucks," Herbie said.

"That's almost three loads," Just Juice added.

"So, you got the money back?" she asked.

"Uh, no. I mean, the next person could have gotten double change," Herbie said.

"So then what?" Elizabeth looked from one man to the other. "You told Squeaky and he gave it back? Or told you too bad?"

Quickly, Just Juice said, "He already went home."

Elizabeth opened her small, spiral notebook. "When was this?"

"Um," Herbie said.

"Lemme see." Just Juice's expression might have been intended to be thoughtful. Elizabeth thought it looked more like a toddler on the potty.

She set her pen on the table with a sharp snap. "I think there could be some things you aren't telling me." She did a gimme gesture with four fingers of her left hand.

"Really," Herbie said, "that's all there is to it."

Elizabeth raised her eyebrows. "On Monday five bucks is a burger and fries at the Bully Pulpit."

"Also Thursday," Just Juice said.

"All the more reason to ask for your money from Squeaky. Convince me that you weren't trying to open the change machine to steal its contents."

Elizabeth listened to ten seconds of indignant denials. "Studied Shakespeare yet?"

"Huh?" Herbie asked.

She stared at each of them in turn. "Me thinketh you protest too much."

Just Juice shifted his heavy frame in his chair. "Honest, Chief. We just wanted our money back."

Elizabeth stood. "I'm sure you'll file for reimbursement with Mr. Miller." She pointed to the door of the conference room. "You can leave."

They stood and moved toward the door, apparently uncertain which one should precede the other through it. When she heard them say goodbye to Sgt. Hammer and close the station door behind them, Elizabeth walked out of the conference room.

Hammer met her in the hallway. "No dice?"

"Dice, I think, but of course they don't want to admit they were trying to break into the machine."

Hammer followed Elizabeth into her office. "They're both so big they could almost block the view from the street. Of the machine, I mean."

She nodded. "And it's partially blocked by a column. I told them to ask Squeaky for a refund, since they said it kept their five-dollar bill. If Squeaky kept better records we'd have something to go on."

"His changer would be five dollars over?" Hammer asked.

"Yep. I think they'll quit trying to break into the changer, but it doesn't really help us with Louella Belle."

Hammer half-shrugged. "Maybe it'll give them an incentive to tell you more later."

CHAPTER FIFTEEN

ELIZABETH HUNG UP HER phone after encouraging the city clerk to take up a collection to get Finn Clancy a bike. She smiled. Dingle really didn't want to do it, but finally agreed.

Before she could think about what to do next, Hammer ran into her office. "Stanley Buttons is dead. At the senior apartments."

"Heart attack?"

"Sort of. A knife stopped his heart."

Only Wednesday and two murders this week? She stood and reached for her jacket and cap and unlocked the file cabinet to retrieve her gun. She had begun to think she should wear it in the station. "Where? In his apartment?"

Hammer stood aside as she strode past him into the bullpen. "In the parking lot. When he didn't come back from the grocery store by dinner time, someone found him."

"Cameras in that lot?" Elizabeth asked.

"They have cameras at the main and side exits, but focused on the areas around the doors. None in the lot."

"Damn. See if you can find Calderone and Mahan. Have them meet me at the apartments."

"With the crime scene kit," Hammer said.

Elizabeth turned on the car's lights and siren and was at the senior apartments in less than two minutes. Grayson beat her there. She wondered if someone had called his cell directly, or if he'd been close and seen the ambulance.

Final Cycle

He walked up as she got out of her car. "It's terrible, Chief. It looks like…"

Elizabeth said, "Don't talk so loud."

He swallowed. "I'm sorry. So hard to see. Looks like he tried to crawl a few feet after he got stabbed. If someone had seen him…"

"We don't know yet if that would have made a difference." She walked quickly toward the ambulance and small firetruck. "We need a broader perimeter Grayson. Set it up."

"Yes, Chief." He pulled a wad of crime scene tape from his jacket pocket.

Elizabeth frowned. At least Grayson had thought of that. She really needed a different person on in the evening.

An EMT gestured that she should come to him. "Chief. Helluva thing." He nodded at the pavement.

Stanley now lay on his back coat unbuttoned, with a defibrillator on the ground near him. It didn't look as if the EMTs had tried to use it.

Elizabeth agreed with Grayson. The man had likely crawled a few paces on his stomach, because the blood trail had two large round spots. Probably from where his chest had rested a couple of times as he crawled.

She glanced at the young EMT, whom she didn't recognize. "Looks like major blood loss."

He nodded, and spoke in a low voice. "The wound is just below the heart, I think. Probably hit an artery. Wool coat absorbed a lot of the blood. He didn't last long."

"You call the ME?"

He nodded. "Skelly said to tell you he'd meet you here, instead of the diner." His look held a question.

Elizabeth smiled briefly. "He has my cat. She got injured today, and he's been keeping an eye on her."

The EMT raised his eyebrows. "What, he's a vet now?"

"Just helping me out." She extended her hand. "Chief Elizabeth Friedman."

"Seen your picture in the paper. Nick Weaver. Just moved here from Springfield." He turned back to the ambulance and the several other EMTs and fire fighters who stood a few feet from Stanley.

Elizabeth did a full rotation, taking in the scene. The seven-story apartments had a smaller parking lot than other complexes of its size. Most of its residents didn't drive. At the far end, close to the street, a row of what she thought were honeysuckle bushes provided a barrier between the sidewalk and parking lot. Even though they had shed most of their leaves, they still obstructed the view from the street into the lot.

She refocused on the area close to her. The cold had kept most onlookers in the apartment building's lobby. Or maybe some had come out and then gone back in. Grace stood between two men, who looked to be in their mid-seventies. The men had on heavy coats, but Grace had wrapped herself in a heavy afghan.

"Why don't you three sit in my car with me? You can get warm." She gestured toward her car, and walked ahead of them. She leaned into the driver's side, turned off its flashing lights, and started the ignition.

She opened the car's back door. "Gentlemen, have a seat. Grace, you'll get warmer faster in the front seat." Elizabeth opened the front passenger door, and watched as one of the men guided Grace into the car. Then he climbed in the back.

Elizabeth got into the driver's seat, shut her door, and turned up the heat before she turned to face them. "If we sit here for a few minutes we can talk quietly." She studied Grace, whose cheeks bore tear tracks. "I'm sorry, Grace."

She dabbed at her nose with a balled tissue. "He asked if I needed anything, and I wanted some red and green sprinkles. You know, for Christmas cookies."

Elizabeth leaned across the seat to grab some tissues from her glove box. She handed Grace one and waved a couple toward the back seat. The men declined.

"I don't believe I've met you gentlemen. Did you find Stanley?"

The man in a black wool coat said, "Herb Schwartz."

The second man, who wore a Green Bay Packers jacket, said, "Arthur Tennenbaum. No, we didn't find him. The apartment receptionist was just leaving when Grace said Stanley should have been back. She, Angela's her name, said she'd stop at the grocery store on her way home, but when she was walking to her car she saw Stanley."

Final Cycle

Elizabeth felt annoyed. She had assumed, always bad form, that she would be questioning the people who found Stanley. "Do you know where Angela went?"

Herb Schwartz said, "We were in the lobby when she came in to call you folks. She said Stan was dead, and she was holding it together, but she was upset."

"Of course," Elizabeth said. "Where is she?"

"She left her phone number at the front desk," Herb said.

Arthur jumped in. "Her husband is diabetic, and she makes sure she's home to fix dinner."

Elizabeth felt her eyebrows go up.

"Her husband's in bed. Lost his foot to diabetes last year."

"I get it," Elizabeth said. "I'll call her in a few minutes. So, she came in from the lot, and you came right out?"

Herb said, "We went down the hall to our apartments to get our coats before we came out."

"Since we couldn't help him," Arthur said.

"Smart," Elizabeth said. "So you were on the scene within what, a couple of minutes?"

"They live on the first floor," Grace said. "I didn't want to go to upstairs to get my coat. I took an afghan from the lobby."

Herb said, "Two, three minutes."

"Did you notice anyone?" she asked.

Both men shook their heads. Arthur added, "Very quiet. Hardly anyone's been out. The lot still has patches of ice."

Grace sobbed into a tissue. "I knew it was bad as soon as Angela hurried back in. I thought maybe Stanley fell."

Two cars pulled into the lot. Elizabeth recognized Mahan's patrol car and Skelly's dark green Camry.

She looked at the threesome. "I need to talk to my officer. How about I pull up to the entrance so you don't have to walk on the ice. Then I'll be back in a few minutes and I'll probably want to talk to you again."

She turned to Grace. "Have you called your daughter?"

Grace shook her head. "My phone's inside."

Elizabeth turned her head toward the back seat. "Can you help Grace get to her phone, and walk her to her apartment to get something warmer?"

"Sure thing," Herb said.

She turned to the steering wheel and put the car in gear. "I or one of my officers will talk to you again tonight. In the meantime, please think about anything you might have noticed in the parking lot, and don't talk to a lot of people."

She pulled to the lobby door as Arthur said, "No cross-contamination, so to speak."

Elizabeth glanced at him via her rear view mirror. "Exactly. You retired law enforcement?"

"No. Department of Agriculture food inspection. Same principles."

Elizabeth figured half of her job now was to calm frightened residents. She quickly got to Grace's passenger door and helped the woman out.

Mahan walked over to her. "Chief?"

"I'm going to talk to the group for just a minute and come out. You know what to do."

He turned back toward the ambulance. "Sure do."

In a weak voice, Grace asked, "What's he going to do?"

"Make sure you're safe."

Automatic doors parted and the four of them entered the now crowded lobby.

Questions poured from the group.

"Is it really Stanley?"

"What happened?"

"Should we stay inside?"

"Is it the same person who killed Louella Belle?"

Arthur and Herb led Grace to an upholstered chair as Elizabeth spoke. "As I think you heard from Angela, she did find Stanley. But I have to ask you not to talk to others about his identity. We have not notified his family."

A man in a wheelchair said, "I called his son in Peoria. He's coming down."

Inwardly, Elizabeth winced. "Before I step back outside, please give me his phone number."

She addressed the group. "When we know anything, I will tell you. In the meantime…"

A woman in expensive-looking green slacks and a cream blouse asked, "When, in six weeks?"

"Genevieve," another woman muttered.

Final Cycle

"I can't give you a timeframe on resolving the situation, but I guarantee I or one of my officers will stop by every day for a while. It's less scary when you know what's going on."

A couple of people said thank you.

"As far as tonight is concerned, I need to go back outside for now. I'd like to give you some things to think about before I come back. Please do me a favor and don't talk a lot about this until you talk to me or Officer Mahan or one of the others."

"Why not?" Genevieve asked.

"I need your *individual* recollections first. Before I go outside, in the last couple of hours, did anyone see a stranger in the building, or the parking lot?"

They looked at one another and said no or shook their heads.

"Okay. Things to think about. Not to tell me this minute. When you last saw or talked to Stanley, if he mentioned whether anyone was angry with him, or whether he was annoyed with anyone. Did Stanley do anything out of his usual routine lately?"

Arthur asked, "May we go to our apartments?"

Elizabeth hesitated. "Briefly, if you need something. For those of you who were in the immediate area when Stanley was found, or if you have something helpful to tell us, please wait in the lobby initially."

She glanced at Arthur. "Sir, maybe you could start a list of names and phone numbers for me."

"Of course."

The man in the wheelchair pulled up to her. "His son is Steven. Number's on the napkin."

Elizabeth thanked him and turned toward the door. She walked back into the cold, trying to decide if she should call Stanley's son when he was on the road. She would think about that for a couple of minutes.

Murder was always horrible, but with Louella Belle's, she could speculate as to motive. Stanley had seemed like a good-natured retiree who would not accumulate enemies. What was going on in Logland?

CHAPTER SIXTEEN

SOMEONE HAD DRIVEN THE ME'S van into the lot and Skelly and another man were lifting Stanley onto a gurney as Elizabeth walked back into the lot. The second man had dark green scrubs under his heavy parka, so Elizabeth figured he had brought the van from the hospital.

Mahan stopped her before she'd gone twenty feet. "Skelly said Stanley had something under three of his fingernails. Can't tell what."

"Let's hope he scratched his killer. Anyone see anything out here?"

Mahan shook his head. "No, and since the lot is in front of the main entrance, the building sits back quite a ways from the street. Unless there'd been a loud struggle, I doubt someone walking a dog would have noticed much."

"Okay. I'll talk to Skelly for a minute." Elizabeth noted all but one ambulance had left and the crime scene tape was spread across several cars. "Take a lot of pictures and check under those cars that are taped. I don't see that we need to keep people out of their vehicles too long."

"Grayson went back to the station to get the good camera," Mahan said.

"You can warm up inside if you want. Tell them I'll be in to talk to them in five minutes and reassure them that you don't see any bad guys lurking out here."

She turned toward the van. The man in scrubs pulled out of the lot as Skelly came toward her.

"If you didn't want to do dinner you should have said so." Skelly's hands were thrust deep into his pockets and he had his arms pulled close, warming himself.

She glanced at his feet. "You have on street shoes. You must be freezing. Why don't you sit in your car for a few minutes and I'll be back out."

"Sounds good." He half-jogged to his car, almost slipping on a patch of ice.

Elizabeth turned toward the apartment entrance. From a distance, it seemed no one had returned to their units.

Grayson pulled into the lot with the camera and Mahan left the building as she entered. After five more minutes with the group, it was clear everyone, even the grouchy Genevieve, considered Stanley affable, always willing to do a favor if someone needed a ride to church or the pharmacy. He had not talked to any of them about people being angry with him or vice versa.

Grace added, "But he didn't let anyone take advantage of him. And if he said he'd give you a ride and you were late, he wouldn't do it again."

"How easy is it to get into this building?" Elizabeth asked.

A frail-looking woman said, "But he was killed outside!"

Arthur said, "She knows, Emily." He turned to Elizabeth. "You've seen the keypad. The security code is changed monthly. Used to be a system to it, month, year, that kind of thing. But someone stole part of the nativity scene last Christmas and…"

"From the lobby," Grace added.

Arthur smiled tightly. "Yes, the lobby. After that, the management company decided to make it random numbers every month."

"And you have no idea what a pain that is," Genevieve said. "Half the people forget the code and then they pound on the door or use the intercom phone to call another resident to get in."

A man who looked about ninety-five chuckled. "Always when I'm napping."

"I haven't seen a manager tonight," Elizabeth said.

"Nobody lives on site," Herb Schwartz said. "It's an independent living building. Desk only staffed during the day. Called the management firm an hour ago."

Elizabeth reminded herself to call the absent receptionist and stopped herself from saying management response time was ridiculously slow. "So, I asked you about ease of getting in because I wondered if people who shouldn't be here often tried to sneak in."

People exchanged glances and shrugged. Finally Grace said. "Mostly people's kids. Sometimes the UPS guy follows one of us in, but we know him."

"Okay, so no sense of stranger danger?"

Several muttered, "Stranger danger."

Arthur's tone was emphatic. "Never. Worst thing that happens around here is the trees get toilet-papered for homecoming and high school graduation."

The ninety-five looking man said, "But if you could keep out the Girl Scouts. I really hate paying that much for cookies."

Elizabeth's sensed he wasn't joking. "Okay. I'm glad it's usually safe. I had wondered if Stanley might have previously confronted someone who wanted to come in and he denied them entry. Would you have heard about that?"

"Probably would have seen it," Arthur said. "Usually a few of us in the lobby."

"What about at a side door?"

Arthur shrugged. "Management says the cameras at the doors are monitored."

"But we don't think they are," Genevieve added. "I stick my tongue out at them a lot, and no one says anything.

"Okay. Arthur, you have that list of names and phone numbers for me?"

He handed it to her.

She took it and put it in an inside pocked of her jacket. "As I said, we'll be over every day, starting tomorrow morning. You can call the station anytime. Media will want to talk to you. That's up to you. All I ask is that if you think of something else, you call me before you tell anyone else."

Elizabeth left the building. She shivered and zipped her jacked to her neck as she walked toward Mahan, who stood next to the remaining ambulance talking to Nick Weaver and Skelly. They stopped talking when she got to them.

"Get warm, Skelly?"

"Not really. Wanted to offer advice on which pictures to take." Skelly tilted his head toward the apartment building. "Hear anything about a weapon, or anything else, in there?"

She shook her head. "Once again, it's all on you."

Mahan cleared his throat and she nodded to him. "And my crackerjack force."

Skelly asked. "You knew Mr. Buttons?"

"Met him a couple of days ago. He was in the laundromat just before we think Louella Belle was killed."

Skelly's eyes widened. "That can't be a coincidence."

Elizabeth glanced at Nick Weaver. "You aren't hearing this conversation."

"Yes, ma'am."

"I'm not a fan of coincidences in law enforcement," Elizabeth said. "Stanley was a nice guy, from what everyone says."

Skelly stomped his feet. "I couldn't do anything here. Cold temperature is good for preservation, but it may make it harder to determine time of death."

Elizabeth nodded. "We know when he left for the store. We'll check and see when he finished there. Should be able to get pretty close to an exact time. I'll call you."

Skelly almost smiled. "I left the cat with your landlady. Neither one of them is happy about it."

WHEN SHE GOT BACK to the station, Calderone met her at the front door. Cheeks red, he looked as if he had just arrived. Hammer spoke on the phone, apparently to a reporter because he kept refusing to identify the victim.

Calderone said, "We went to dinner, I just..."

Elizabeth waved a hand. "Mostly done at the apartments. Grayson should be back with the camera soon. Mahan heard about it and he came down."

Hammer hung up. "People seem to know it was Stanley Buttons."

"Everyone in the building knew, and they probably called their families. I want to talk to his son before we confirm to media. He's supposedly driving down from Peoria." She pointed toward her office. "Let's talk in there. Jerry Pew should be by, if he hasn't already."

Hammer stood from his desk. "I got back in here about forty minutes ago. Haven't seen him."

"Bowling banquet tonight," Calderone said. "They usually invite him."

"Free food for Jerry." Elizabeth pulled the soggy napkin from her pocket. When they got to her office she picked up the phone as the men sat. "I didn't try the son because he's driving. He hasn't called here, has he?"

Hammer shook his head. "Only messages on the machine were media. Oh, and Dingle and the mayor. You need to call them."

Elizabeth acknowledged with a nod and began to punch buttons.

A man's harsh voice answered. "Who is this?"

"Chief Elizabeth Friedman in Logland."

"Why the hell haven't you called me before now?"

"My assumption was you'd be driving. If you are, please pull over and we'll talk for a minute. I'm sorry about your father." Elizabeth punched the speaker button.

She covered the mouthpiece and whispered. "His name's Steven. Someone at the apartment called him more than an hour ago."

Unintelligible muttering came through the phone. Finally, Steven said. "I pulled off I-55."

"Thanks. We don't need two Buttons men dying tonight. I wish a resident had not called you, but when I realized you already knew, I spent some time investigating. Sometimes people wander away and you lose access to them." Elizabeth didn't add that a slow possum could keep up with the seniors she'd spoken to.

"Okay. Well. What the hell happened to my father?"

"It seems he was accosted in the apartment's parking lot. He'd been to the grocery store, and when he didn't return for dinner, someone checked the lot. Once he'd been found, help came quickly, but I'm sorry to say he'd already passed."

"Do you know who did it?"

"No." Elizabeth glanced at Calderone and Hammer. "I have several people questioning folks, but we aren't starting with a suspect list."

Steven Buttons' seething came through the phone. "And why not?"

"Because your father seems to have been well-liked. In fact, I met him just the other day."

"Oh, right. Are you the lady cop who talked to him after the loudmouth woman was killed in the laundry place?"

Hammer put his forehead in his hand and Calderone looked at the ceiling.

"I am she," Elizabeth said. "At that time, he didn't think he'd seen anything that would indicate who the killer of Louella Belle Simpson was. He didn't happen to discuss it with you, did he?"

"He called me the night you talked to him, and again last night. It rattled him."

Calderone and Hammer sat up straighter. Hammer grabbed a piece of paper from a pad on Elizabeth's desk and took a pen from his breast pocket.

"Besides letting you know he was upset, did your father mention anyone who may have bothered him, anything like that?"

"He said he'd decided not to go there anymore because, and these were his words, 'Several lowlifes hang out there.' Do you know who he meant?"

Elizabeth hesitated for two seconds. "I know of one for sure, but we verified his alibi for Louella Belle. A couple of times. Did he mention any names?"

"No, damn it. And I didn't ask."

"Did he mention anyone in his apartment building he didn't get along with?" Elizabeth asked.

"Not that I remember. Couple old biddies he tried to avoid, but not because he was afraid of them. One lady was real deaf and shouted every conversation."

Calderone silently mouthed "old biddies."

Elizabeth grimaced. "Mr. Buttons, the weather isn't good, and you can't do much here tonight. If you're tired, why don't you stop at a motel for the night?"

Steven Buttons' voice cracked. "I should have moved him up to Peoria."

"He seemed happy here. I'm sorry he died as he did."

Buttons agreed and ended the call.

Elizabeth looked at Hammer and Calderone. "Bad things can happen anywhere, but why twice here in three days?"

CHAPTER SEVENTEEN

THURSDAY MORNING ELIZABETH stopped at a McDonalds and bought eight one-dollar breakfast sandwiches. Better for thinking than donuts. Which she saw Hammer had bought and placed on his desk in the bullpen.

"Morning, Chief."

"Not a very good one." She put the bag of sandwiches next to the donuts.

"Smells good. Mayor called."

"Thanks." In her office, Elizabeth shrugged out of her coat and picked up the phone on her desk. She dialed city hall and the mayor herself picked up.

"Elizabeth, I mean Chief, thanks for calling before everyone gets in this morning."

"I don't know more than I did when we talked for a minute last night. Skelly has Stanley, and we'll check cameras at the senior apartments. Don't think they'll show much."

"Why not?" she asked.

"They don't encompass much of the parking lot. My officers will check residences near the apartment building. Not a lot of people in town have security cameras, but there's a chance a nearby one may have caught someone running away."

Mayor Harmon lowered her voice. "You think it relates to Louella Belle's murder?"

"Hard not to think that, but we'll look at any options. His son is coming down from Peoria. You'll talk to him if he wants to, right?"

"Oh, dear. Of course. Please call as soon as you know anything."

Elizabeth assured her she would. "Could you have Mr. Dingle call me?"

"Why?"

"He knows a lot of people who live in the building." A white lie, or maybe he did know a lot of people. Elizabeth wanted to press Dingle again on what he had asked Louella Belle to do. And see if he'd collected money for a replacement bike for Finn Clancy.

Her phone buzzed as she hung up, and Hammer said, "Jerry Pew for you."

"Jerry. Thought we might see you last night."

"Wish you'da called me," he groused.

"Doesn't work that way. I told the apartment residents you'd probably call."

"What the hell happened to Stanley Buttons? The online police blotter said he was found dead in the parking lot of 'apparent stab wounds.' Who killed him?"

"Did you ever send over that list of suspects you had for could've killed Louella Belle?" Elizabeth asked.

The editor said nothing.

"We have no suspects, Jerry. He'd been to the grocery store and didn't come back to dinner. He was found in the parking lot." She carefully didn't say who'd found him, and made a mental note to ask Mahan what the apartment receptionist had told him.

"I haven't talked to the guy since he retired. Did a story on some class of his sometime. Don't remember what. Didn't seem like an a-hole."

"Nice people get murdered, too, Jerry. I have to go."

"Wait a minute, Chief! I'm at deadline. I had the story about Louella Belle, but now we've got Stanley Buttons. What the hell is going on in Logland?"

She chose her words carefully, knowing he would quote her. "Stanley Buttons' death is a real tragedy, but we don't have a link to Louella Belle's murder. We will be vigorously investigating both."

"Chief, it's almost Christmas and we have two murders."

Elizabeth said nothing.

"Chief?"

"I didn't hear a question, Jerry."

"Damn it, I want to know what the hell's going on. The only time we've had two deaths so close together was if there was a car accident."

"I wish I could tell you more, but as you know, Mr. Buttons was only killed yesterday evening."

"Do you have any suspects?"

"Not as of yet. I really need to get back to the investigation, Jerry. Why don't you touch base with Sergeant Hammer later today?"

"But I gotta get to press in an hour or I can't have the paper ready for tomorrow morning."

"Mr. Pew, I think you know that if I had more information for the citizens of Logland, I would give it to you." She hung up.

Elizabeth grabbed a sandwich from Hammer's desk. "I'll talk to the mayor or any city or county official. Can you handle the public?"

"Sure. Jerry Pew's gonna say you hung up on him."

She grinned. "You're my witness. I simply ended the call because he wouldn't stop talking." More seriously, she added, "I'll talk to Buttons' son, Steven. So will the mayor. Did that building management company ever get in touch?"

"They're pulling video. I told them not to edit any of it. They'll send a digital file."

Calderone and Mahan came in from the station's back entrance. Elizabeth could hear them putting coats in the locker room. She turned to Hammer. "Have them meet in my office. Join us. You can answer the phone from there."

BY NINE O'CLOCK THURSDAY MORNING, they had divvied up interviews, but Elizabeth didn't expect to learn anything from talking to Stanley's acquaintances. At best maybe they could identify the low lifes he'd mentioned to his son.

"Mahan," Elizabeth said, "you talked to the woman who found him."

He nodded. "Very upset. Kept saying how nice he was. She didn't see anyone else in the parking lot." He consulted his notes.

"Before the EMTs got there of course. So he was on his stomach, head turned to the right."

"And no movement of any kind?" Elizabeth asked.

"No. She noticed the blood stains, from where he maybe tried to crawl a couple feet. That upset her the most. You can't really understand her when she talks about that."

"Damn shame," Hammer said.

"I want to talk to Finn Clancy again," Calderone said. "They both went to the laundromat."

"We need a reason besides Clancy's a creep who hung out at the laundromat," Elizabeth said.

"Good enough for me," Mahan muttered.

"I don't want him accusing us of harassment. He'd love for Jerry Pew to do a story on that. But," Elizabeth nodded toward Calderone, "ask him if he noticed anything around town about the time Stanley was killed. Tell him we're asking because he's out and about a lot."

"Where does he sleep?" Hammer asked.

"Sometimes the Mission," Calderone said. "When it's cold. When the campground outside of town is open, he pitches a tent there a lot."

"Where does he get money for that?" Elizabeth asked.

Calderone shrugged. "How much is it?"

"I think it's at least $15 for a tent spot," Hammer said. "For $450 a month he could get a room in one of those old motels that pretend they're apartments now."

"Is he on some kind of disability?" Elizabeth asked.

"For what?" Mahan asked. "They don't give disability income for being lazy."

"Maybe depression," Elizabeth said. "Seems someone who chooses his lifestyle might be. I don't suppose you can just call social services without a warrant."

"I'll ask around," Calderone said. "He has to have money from somewhere. He doesn't beg on the corners."

"He plays a lot of pool," Hammer said. "Those guys all bet with each other. Maybe he wins."

Mahan said, "Hard to imagine. I stopped at the grocery store. Employees who saw Stanley last night aren't there this morning. Manager wouldn't give me phone numbers, but he's giving them my cell number."

"Jeez," Elizabeth said. "Why the hell not?"

"Some company policy about employee privacy. I told him to have them to call me soon. He also said Louella Belle was in there a few weeks ago, wanting him to put up signs on the bulletin board about food allergies. He feels bad he ignored her."

Elizabeth shook her head. "I don't feel good about solving this. Unless Stanley did have someone's skin under his nails and there's a DNA match. We know how long that'll take."

"Poor old guy," Hammer said. The phone rang and he answered it, then nodded at Elizabeth. "Yes, sir. Just a moment." He put the call on hold. "Dingle."

Calderone and Mahan stood, Hammer handed Elizabeth the phone and the three men walked out.

"Thanks for calling, Mr. Dingle."

In a more cordial tone than he usually had for her, Dingle said, "Mayor mentioned you thought I might know a lot of the residents in the senior apartments."

"If you do and hear any talk that seems relevant, I'd like to know that. Mostly I need to know two other things. One, any luck on collecting funds for a bike for Finn Clancy, and two, any more thoughts on what Louella Belle may have discovered for you at the laundromat?"

Dingle cleared this throat. "One hundred nine dollars."

"Maybe the hardware store will have a used one. How about Louella Belle? Did you think of anything?"

"Honest to God, no, Chief. She only went in there a couple of times. Mostly only said Squeaky didn't sweep well, because a lot of lint collected in the corners, and some little kids left small plastic baggies near the trash cans."

Elizabeth sat up straighter. "Why did she think they were kids' baggies?"

"Tiny. Louella Belle said like you could get from a hobby shop, for coins or beads. They had cartoon drawings stamped on them."

"Do you have any of them?" Elizabeth asked.

"No, why? I had the impression she tossed them and was going to chew out Squeaky."

"Thanks, Mr. Dingle. I'll stop by for the contributions, or one of the officers will. Appreciate it."

Before a sputtering Dingle could ask more, Elizabeth hung up. She called, "Hey, Hammer. You out there?"

He pushed back his chair in the bullpen and quickly rounded the corner from that room into the hallway. "What's up, Chief?"

"Dingle said Louella Belle told him she found some," Elizabeth made air quotes, "tiny baggies that must have belonged to children because they had pictures on them."

"Damn. Dime bags. Did Dingle know what drugs had been in them?"

"The moron really thought they were kids' bags." She stood.

Hammer stared at her.

"Okay," Elizabeth said. "I shouldn't call the city clerk a moron."

"Fine by me. I'm thinking about who else we could ask about that. Everyone keeps saying they didn't see anything unusual in the laundromat."

Elizabeth came from behind her desk. "I'm going to talk to Squeaky again."

TEN MINUTES LATER, SQUEAKY was all shrugs. "Chief, I saw one on the back stoop of the laundromat, one time. Figured it blew there."

"What marking was on it?"

"I'm sorry, Chief. I didn't pick it up. Pink blob all's it looked like to me. Or maybe red."

Squeaky unlocked his cash drawer. "Got a bunch of people picking up dry cleaning today. You know, for Christmas."

"Mr. Miller," Elizabeth said.

He looked up, startled. "Chief, if people were selling drugs while they did their laundry, I never heard about it. I woulda told you."

When Elizabeth continued to stare at him, Squeaky asked, "What were they selling?"

"I have no idea. I always figure some of that goes on at the college, but unless it spills into town, I don't focus on it."

Final Cycle

Without saying goodbye, Elizabeth turned and walked into the bone-chilling cold. Knowing about the baggies three days ago could have helped them at least target suspicion on drug sales. Could mean nothing, could mean Louella Belle saw a sale in progress and was killed to keep her mouth shut. *What a waste.*

She turned on the heater in the Crown Vic and pulled her phone from a pocket. She knew one person who could know what drugs were sold on campus.

Wally Kermit picked up immediately. "I was going to call you, Chief. What's a good time Christmas Eve?"

For a second, Elizabeth didn't associate his question with her earlier invitation to stop by the station that afternoon. "Oh, uh, any time after perhaps two. I have a different topic. You can't blab about it."

She described what she had just learned, with minimal detail. Let him think it was one baggie one time. Or maybe it was only one day.

After silence of several seconds, Wally said, "We don't see as much of that as you might at a larger school. Or one in a big city. At Sweathog, usually it's pot, far as I know."

"But what color, what image, would be stamped on the baggies?"

"Pigs, of course. Usually pink. Sometimes red."

"What's the difference?" Elizabeth asked. "Kind of drugs?"

"What I hear is colors mean who provides the stuff. But like I said, I haven't seen the baggies but two or three times. Homecoming weekend twice. Oh, and last week of school last year. But never more than a couple. And near trash cans. I kinda figured they blew out."

"In the same place each time?"

"Nah. I don't know if it means there's not a lot of drug stuff, or if people know how to clean up after themselves."

Elizabeth hung up and called to Hammer. He came in, cup of coffee in hand. "What's up, Chief?"

"Squeaky says he's only seen one bag and it was on the stoop by the alley. Good old Wally says there's not much activity on campus. He thinks it's all pot."

He sat across from her desk. "So, doesn't tell us much, I guess."

"Wally did say that what Squeaky thought were paint smudges of pink or red were likely of pigs, and the colors designate who's selling what."

"Sure, same as gangs in the cities." He grinned. "Bet the ones at Sweathog are the only ones with pigs on them."

"No doubt. Start a list. Our buddies Herbie and Just Juice. Clancy. And...Blake Wessley acts like he really cleaned up his act, but maybe not."

"Could be anyone who used the laundromat," Hammer said.

Elizabeth remembered the two men who'd been in the diner. "Did you find out who those two men were? From the diner, when Skelly and I had lunch."

He pulled a small notebook from the breast pocket of his uniform shirt. "Yeah, I asked Nick. Sorry, found out late yesterday, and then Buttons happened." He flipped a few pages. "You were right about the packing plant. Ted Nelson and Randy Judd."

"We've never arrested them?"

"Nope. They were witnesses to a fight at that grungy bar near the railroad tracks. 'Stop By Here,' it's called."

"Incidents elsewhere?"

He shrugged. "Not what you'd call big stuff. The kinds of things people on the margins get into. Couple shoplifting charges in Peoria for one, bar fight in Decatur for the other."

"So, people you wouldn't want for next-door neighbors, but nothing serious."

"And no guns used, ever. Neither has a concealed carry permit."

Elizabeth blew out air. "But unless they're felons or convicted of domestic violence, they could probably both get one."

"If they take the safety class," Hammer said.

She nodded. "They probably never crossed paths with Louella Belle or Stanley. They don't deserve to be on our radar just because they look rough. As we talk to more people about the laundromat, ask them to describe some of the customers they don't know."

Hammer swallowed the last of his coffee. "They could have gun owners' permits. I'll check the state Firearm Owners Identification registry."

When he left, Elizabeth stared at her phone without really seeing it. Her instinct said they were looking for an aggressor who wouldn't appear on any lists for past behavior or weapons ownership. Killers who flew under the radar could hide in plain sight.

CHAPTER EIGHTEEN

THOUGH HAMMER SAID MARTI had called the station a couple of times to see if they'd arrested anyone, Elizabeth hadn't talked to her in depth since Monday evening.

She headed for the Bully Pulpit before the Thursday lunch rush. Maybe a calmer Marti, or at least one a few days past her discovery of Louella Belle, would remember more if Elizabeth prodded her a little.

As she opened the door to enter the diner, Elizabeth absorbed that in the three days since the murder, the Bully Pulpit had exploded in Christmas colors and – no other word for it – tacky decorations. She unzipped her jacket and headed for a booth midway into the diner. *What could Marti and Nick have possibly been thinking?*

Marti's voice carried in from the kitchen and moved closer. "So, I think if we went to the hardware store they'd probably just give us some of the leftover live garland. Don't you think it would smell really good?"

Nick's response was muffled.

The swinging door that led to the kitchen opened and Marti rounded the corner, coffee pot in hand. Elizabeth hadn't seen other patrons, but figured they must be around the corner, in the longer end of the L shape.

Marti stopped when she saw Elizabeth and her eyebrows went up. "Chief! Do you know anything?"

She shook her head. "Learning more all the time, but we haven't identified anyone yet."

Marti's shoulders sagged. "That would be a great Christmas present. Then I wouldn't have to worry anymore."

"What are you...?"

"Chief, let me take this coffee to Gordon Beals. He's around the corner there.""

Elizabeth nodded. The insurance actuary had just returned from a long visit to an older sister in Phoenix. He referred to it as his winter solace.

She opened a menu and a doily that had been colored as a Christmas wreath fell out. Nick peered around the cash register, which sat on the counter in front of the swinging door. He placed a finger to his lips and gestured that Elizabeth should come to the counter.

Marti's loud laugh said she was still busy with Beals, so Elizabeth walked to Nick. "What is it?"

"You have to get her to stop this."

"Stop what?" she asked.

He pointed to the diner's ceiling, from which hung a bunch of small, homemade mobiles, each telling part of either the Nativity story or Santa's workshop. "She can't stop doing crafts and stuff. Two days ago she asked every patron to bring her art stuff so she could decorate."

"Ah. It is, uh, overwhelming."

In a harsh whisper, Nick said, "No kidding!"

Marti's rapid footsteps approached, and Elizabeth turned. "I was just asking Nick who had made all these wonderful decorations. They look new."

Marti stopped at the counter and placed the coffee pot on it. "I'm so excited about Christmas. I've stayed up until after three the last two mornings. I have so many ideas."

Nick's grin was feeble. "I gotta stir the chile." He turned and entered the kitchen.

Softly, Elizabeth said, "It's all beautiful. But don't wear yourself out. Don't you cook a special lunch on Christmas Eve?"

"Oh, right." Marti took her menu pad from an apron pocket. "I keep forgetting what I want to buy."

Elizabeth tilted her head toward the booth where she'd left her jacket. "Take a break and sit with me for a second."

Marti's shoulders sagged. "Do we have to talk about...it?"

Elizabeth shook her head, firmly. "No. I thought we'd chat for a minute. I'd love to hear what you're doing for Christmas." *Or whether I should suggest a rest and valium.*

Marti slid into the booth across from Elizabeth, back to the kitchen, worry lines forming in her face. "Do you think the person will come after me?"

For someone who didn't want to talk about Louella Belle's murder, Marti had gotten to it quickly. Elizabeth shook her head. "You saw nothing. No doubt the killer was gone quite some time before you walked over to the laundromat."

She leaned back in the booth. "Nick keeps telling me that." He eyes swept the portion of the diner in front of her. "I wish I could believe it."

"If you could help your mind unwind, I think you'd feel safer. You'd know the person doesn't want anything to do with you."

Marti's eyes filled. "Every time I shut my eyes I see Louella Belle."

Elizabeth reached across the table and placed one hand over Marti's. "That's natural. You had a terrible shock in a place you thought was safe."

Marti leaned across the table. "Yes! Yes! That's why it bothers me so much." She lay her head on folded arms on the booth's tabletop and began to sob.

A man's voice from behind them said, "Oh, crap."

Elizabeth kept her hand on Marti's, and looked over her shoulder at Gordon Beals. "She'll be okay, Gordon."

Every inch of his six-foot plus frame said he didn't want to offer to help. "Marti, kiddo, can I do something for you?"

Without lifting her head, she said, "No, thank you." Big sniff. "No charge for the coffee."

Gordon smiled slightly at Elizabeth. "I left you a Christmas tip on my table."

Marti lifted her head. "Th..thank you."

Apparently alarmed by her blotchy face and tear-stained cheeks, Gordon said, "Merry Christmas." He hurried out the diner's door into the cold.

Marti grabbed a wad of napkins from the holder on the table. "Gordon'll never come back."

"Sure he will. He likes you. I bet he left a big tip."

She sniffed loudly. "He and Ben were good friends."

"Yes," Elizabeth said. "And even though Ben is gone, he still comes to the Bully Pulpit."

Marti took another napkin and blotted her eyes.

"It doesn't look really busy, Marti. I saw you guys put a recliner in the large food pantry in the back of the kitchen. Why don't you take a nap?"

"Oh, I don't know..." She glanced behind her, toward the kitchen.

"Nick won't mind."

She slid to the edge of the booth bench. "He won't. He's been saying I should go home." She stood and looked down at Elizabeth. "Thanks, Chief. I feel better."

As she walked into the kitchen, Nick called to her. "Marti, you want me to go get some garland?"

Her voice carried into the seating area. "No, I think we have enough decorations."

Elizabeth slipped back into her jacket and stood. No more information from Marti.

BEFORE GOING BACK TO THE station, Elizabeth stopped by the hardware store. It always amused her that the best window decorations in town were done by the same people who sold smelly fertilizer in the spring.

This year an almost life-sized elf sat in the middle of a large table, with a train in constant, encircling motion. When she looked more closely at the town that had sprung up around the train just this year, she noted that most of the businesses were those of Logland.

She entered the store and glanced around for the owner to tell him she liked the display.

From behind her, Mike O'Halloran called, "So Chief, you over here to cause trouble?"

She faced him and grinned. "Depends. Is that train out there maintaining proper speed for rural tracks?"

He laughed, which made his perpetually red cheeks turn crimson. "I think we forgot to put up crossing signals. How can I help you?"

"Hammer said he called to see if you had any refurbished bikes. We have to keep one in storage in case we need it as evidence."

He waved toward the back of the store. "One of the guys told me about that. He pulled out two for you to look at." O'Halloran lowered his voice as they walked. "Good of you to do buy one for the Clancy fellow."

Elizabeth noted the two aisles of Christmas trees and decorations still had half-stocked shelves. She could use a wreath for her door. It could take the focus off the hard plastic Mahan had used to replace her broken glass.

"We are hanging onto his main form of transportation for evidence."

O'Halloran pushed open the swinging door that led to the huge storage area behind the main store. "One of these is new. It got scratched when someone test drove it, and hasn't sold. I can give it to you for whatever Hammer said you collected."

"That's very generous of you." She followed the direction of O'Halloran's outstretched hand and took in the man's bike with its black fenders and slim seat. She knew nothing about buying bicycles. This one looked fine. "Sold."

"I won't offer to gift-wrap, but we'll double check tire pressure. Tell Mr. Clancy to stop by. We're open until three o'clock Christmas Eve."

Elizabeth bought a wreath and then drove back to the station. She thought about Stanley Buttons. His son hadn't stopped by the station yet. She wished she could report progress.

ELIZABETH ATE LUNCH AT her desk Thursday as she went over notes on every interview. When she was done, she reviewed digital video from the apartment's entrances. Because of the cameras' positions, most showed people from the neck up. No camera showed the parking lot.

Genevieve did indeed stick out her tongue at the cameras. A woman in a pale blue, angora wool stocking cap didn't look at the camera, but did show it her middle finger every time she entered. *She looks like a fun neighbor.*

Final Cycle

Just before one PM Steven Buttons came to the station. He had maintained his seething disposition. "Chief, why is there crime scene tape on my father's apartment door?"

Elizabeth gestured to a chair across from her desk. "I want to have one of my officers accompany you to go through it. There could be something that mentions a recent appointment or who knows what that could tell us something relevant."

"What if I don't want you to be in there?"

Elizabeth shrugged. "Take me a couple hours to get a warrant. Seems like a waste of time, but if you prefer it, we can get one."

Steven Buttons' six-foot frame sagged in the chair. "It seems like the ultimate violation, going through his things."

"We'll be careful and, as I said, you can be there."

Buttons spread his hands, as if in resignation. "What are you looking for?"

"If he kept a calendar, there could be something that's not routine. I'm not interested in his finances, per se, but if he had recently written a few checks to someone you don't know, maybe a scam artist had been bilking him. Anything out of the ordinary."

Buttons frame was as thin as his father's, and he didn't fill half of the chair. "You don't think it relates to the woman's murder?"

Elizabeth nodded. "I would be surprised if it *isn't* related to Ms. Simpson's death – in some way. But I'm not going to limit our inquiries to that."

"What way?" Steven asked.

"I wish I knew. I wonder if he saw something, maybe not something that meant anything to him, but that the killer wanted your father to forget. Permanently."

"Will you be the one to go through the apartment with me?"

"I'd like to designate Sergeant Hammer, whom you met when you came in. He's very detail-oriented, and he knows this town well. I'm relatively new. Something might jump out at him that I wouldn't see as significant."

When Steven said nothing, Elizabeth asked, "You have any more thoughts about low-lifes your father might have been referring to?"

He slowly shook his head. "I should have paid more attention to him."

SKELLY CALLED JUST BEFORE TWO PM to say the autopsy revealed little. "Have you talked to his son yet?"

"Just did. Stanley hadn't talked about any problems. Hammer's going over to Stanley's apartment with him to see if anything jumps out at them."

"How about his health?"

Elizabeth frowned. "Besides the knife holes?"

"Jeez. No. I wondered if his son knew that Stanley had pretty advanced prostate cancer?"

"He certainly didn't mention it. Is that why he was so thin?"

"I think he was naturally thin, but he had a gaunt look about him. I don't see obvious signs of treatment, but I'm no expert on all aspects of radiation treatment. I wanted a sense of how the son would react when he sees that in the autopsy report."

"My guess is it'll be a surprise. He," Elizabeth hesitated, "would have died in the next year or so?"

"Maybe sooner. Not that it's much comfort at this point, but could be some. I swabbed his fingernails. Probably skin under them, but no blood. If he scratched someone it's likely a faint scratch."

"You're just full of good news, Mr. Medical Examiner."

"What are you cooking Christmas Eve?"

Elizabeth laughed. "Now I'm cooking?"

"Sure. Tell me what and I'll know what kind of wine and catnip to bring."

As Elizabeth hung up the phone, Mahan stuck his head in her office. "Finn Clancy's here. I called him and he picked up the bike. I think he wants to thank you."

"I'll come out there." She followed Mahan and almost laughed when she saw that Clancy had brought the bike into the station."

He wore a heavy jacket in what Elizabeth thought of as hunters' colors, and a smile. "Chief. You got me a bike."

"A bunch of people kicked in. Actually, City Clerk Dingle collected a lot at City Hall." Elizabeth hoped Clancy would feel obliged to bother Dingle.

"I rode it over here from the hardware store. Rides perfect." He grinned. "I bought me a bike lock, too."

"Good idea. My guess is that your old bike will have aged out of service by the time we can get it back to you."

"And then some," Mahan said.

"Anyway, I wanted to say thanks. And I'm sorry I was kinda grouchy with you about keeping the old one."

"No worries. Merry Christmas," Elizabeth said.

Clancy trundled the bike out the entrance to the station, managing to bump the door jamb only once.

HAMMER RETURNED TO THE station at four-thirty, having finished going through Stanley Buttons' apartment with his son. He dropped into a chair across from Elizabeth's desk. "Nothing that either of us could see. The son got all choked up because the table next to his father's recliner had a bunch of old family photo albums, like he'd been going through them."

Elizabeth didn't comment on the albums, but wondered if Stanley knew he had a cancer diagnosis and was reliving the good times in his life. "Stanley was of an age that he might have had checkbooks with carbons rather than used online banking."

"You're right. We went through a couple books of check carbons, which took us back four months. Steven's going to look through more and let us know if he sees anything odd."

Elizabeth stood." I didn't expect a demand for money or anything, but I kind of hoped the person who sent me bricks had mailed Stanley a note."

CHAPTER NINETEEN

ELIZABETH AWOKE FRIDAY morning with her cat's face at her nose. She stroked its head. "Do you feel a lot better?"

Her meow indicated she wanted food, so Elizabeth filled her bowl with dry food. The cat stared at her.

"I gave you soft food last night because you were getting over your boo-boo." The cat stared, but Elizabeth decided to see if she would eat the dry food. Within a minute, chowing down started.

She put on a small pot of coffee and walked onto the landing outside her door to retrieve the paper. When she saw Jerry Pew's story in the Friday morning paper, she wished she kept wine in the house.

Two Murders in Three Days!
Logland Becomes Southern Illinois Murder Capital

Police report no progress in solving the murders of Louella Belle Simpson, which occurred in the Logland Laundromat on Monday evening, or Stanley Buttons, which occurred in the parking lot of the senior apartments Wednesday, in early evening.

Police Chief Elizabeth Friedman said, "Stanley Buttons' death is a real tragedy, but we don't have a link to Louella Belle Simpson's murder. We will be vigorously investigating both."

Elizabeth fumed. She'd talked to Jerry every time he showed up at the station or called. No point in doing that if he tried to make it sound as if she spoke like a press release.

Final Cycle

The article got the chronology of events in the right order, but moved into speculation when it brought up the flyer Louella Belle had done featuring Assistant Principal Maxwell's children.

While no motive is clear in either crime, retired home-ec and health teacher Simpson was known for her passion about what she deemed proper eating habits. She would even walk up to shoppers to suggest that they remove items from their grocery carts and replace them with fresh food.

Her most egregious attempt to sway public opinion was a recent flyer that described some foods as poison and featured local schoolchildren she deemed to be especially well-fed.

Jerry Pew had then inserted a photo of the infamous Louella Belle flyer, with the Maxwell children's heads blotted out.

Aloud, Elizabeth said, "Good God. You'll feel the wrath of Avery Maxwell."

Elizabeth's home phone rang. She answered it with eyes still on the article.

"Uh, Chief? It's Hammer. Listen, I came in early, and there are about twenty voice mails for us. Mostly for you. Some are scared folks, some want to know if we have a vague idea how to catch killers. And they go south from there."

"Thanks, Hammer. I'll get to the station in about half-an-hour." She hung up, sped through her shower, and reached the office in twenty-five minutes.

Calderone sat at Hammer's desk. "He'll be right back. Needed a break from the harsh words."

Elizabeth took off her coat and picked up the two sheets of paper on which Hammer had jotted notes about the messages and phone numbers for return calls. "Can we retain the messages for a couple days in case I want to personally listen to them?"

He nodded. "Digital files. You want me to make copies or something?"

"Do you know how?"

"Heck no, but like you always say, you can teach us old dogs new tricks."

Elizabeth winced. "I'll choose better words next time. I would only want a voice record if one of them is a threat, or maybe a suggested avenue to investigate."

"None of the latter yet. A few insults."

"I can live with those." Elizabeth made copies of the two pages and returned the original to Hammer's desk. As she was about to enter her office to go over the list, Hammer called to her from down the hall.

"Hey Chief, sorry I left my post for a few minutes."

"Stressful times, no problem." She waited a few seconds.

Hammer paused a few feet from her. "The one that really got to me was from that lady, Grace. She just sobs about how we need to catch Stanley's killer." Hammer's voice caught and he stopped.

"If that didn't sadden us, I'd be worried." She tried to make her smile encouraging. "I'll go through this list and return a few calls personally, including Grace's. I'll mark what I do."

"Sounds good, Chief."

Elizabeth placed the list on her desk, grabbed her second cup of coffee, and returned to her office to study the calls. About half of the twenty messages expressed fear, and nearly all of those asked for a call back. One said all downtown businesses should close at dark "to be safe," and another suggested armed security guards at the senior apartment building.

"Oh, good," she muttered. "We can have shoot-outs."

Her personal least favorite was one that said Logland had been safer "before we got a lady police chief." Hammer noted he couldn't discern if a man or woman left the message because the voice appeared to be disguised.

The person left no name, and Elizabeth chuckled when she saw the number that Hammer wrote next to it – she recognized Donald Dingle's home number. *The old guy probably doesn't know that voicemail has caller ID.*

She made several calls to the people who expressed fear, assuring them that the Logland Police Department was actively seeking the killer or killers.

A youngish-sounding woman asked, "Do you think it's safe to let my kids walk to school, when the Christmas holidays are over?"

"If I had kids, I would let them," she answered. "I don't have any reason to think these crimes were random, and they didn't involve children."

Elizabeth left Grace's return call for last.

Grace quavered "Good morning."

"Grace, it's Chief Elizabeth Friedman. I called to check on you. I'm sorry this is such a sad time for you."

"Oh, Chief. I shouldn't have left that message. I couldn't sleep, and I'm just so worried..." Her voice trailed off.

"You can leave a message anytime, Grace. I know Officer Mahan is going to stop by your building around nine-thirty for an update. If you want to be in the lobby for that he'll do his best to answer any questions. The one you'll most want answered, who killed Stanley, he can't tell you yet, I'm afraid."

"We all appreciate that your officers come by. Sergeant Hammer stopped by on his way home last night, just to say hello when a bunch of us were still in the dining room."

Elizabeth swallowed. "He's a good man. One of us will call you personally when we know something. And we will find out who did this to your good friend."

Grace's nose became stuffy. "Thank you, Chief. Merry Christmas."

Elizabeth's phone had been in its cradle for less than five seconds when the intercom buzzed. Hammer said, "Avery Maxwell is on the phone, and she is peeved times four."

"Thanks. I'll take it." She punched the lit button. "Mrs. Maxwell."

The assistant principal's voice shook. "I can't tell you how angry I am with Jerry Pew."

"Me, too. I'm going to call him to say I don't give a tinker's damn about what he says about me or this department, but I'll file a complaint with some journalism professional society if he doesn't get parental permission for any picture that could let kids be identified."

"Oh, good. Is there a law against it? Or implying that the parents of the unidentified kids might have a motive for Louella Belle's murder?"

"I don't know the intricacies of privacy laws, but I believe some journalist code of ethics says to avoid identifying kids, other than in a news story or something, where it's relevant. Even then, not if they're victims, of course."

Her anger welled. "Well, I think he's victimizing my kids!"

"Why don't you call and tell him that, and I'll follow up in an hour or so? We'll double-team him."

Maxwell expelled a breath. "Thank you. Are you having any luck...I mean, do you know who killed either of those people?"

"Not yet, but we're following leads and we aren't letting up."

Maxwell's tone grew business-like. "I have every confidence you'll succeed."

Elizabeth hung up and pulled the folder on Stanley's death toward her. In some ways, returning the phone calls, which had taken almost forty minutes, could be considered a waste of time. But, calming citizens was part of her job.

Donald Dingle was another matter. After the holidays she'd put in a request for another officer, and mention the need for someone who could relate to all ages and both sexes. That would give him something to stew about.

Stanley's file now included notes from interviews with the two young clerks at the Hy-Vee. One had checked out Stanley, another had helped him find the red and green sprinkles Grace had asked him to buy for her.

Neither thought he seemed upset, and they didn't notice that anyone followed him to his car. Because it was dinnertime, the store had few customers.

The female clerk had one observation, which Calderone had typed as a direct quote. "One guy left without buying anything. I don't know his name, but I've seen him before. He doesn't usually leave empty-handed."

Elizabeth stared at the wall opposite her desk. Plenty of reasons to walk out without groceries – a wallet left at home, an item out of stock. But a shopper who left without a purchase could also have wanted to follow someone to the lot.

She walked to the bullpen. "Hammer, is Calderone around?"

"Took a patrol car to drive around the square and a couple streets. Increased presence and all that. Need something?"

"No, but when he comes in I'd like to talk to him about the grocery clerks he interviewed. The ones who were in the store when Stanley shopped that night."

Hammer's expression invited her to say more, but Elizabeth returned to her office. Calderone's notes of the conversation didn't give a detailed description of the man who left empty-handed, only that he was "probably early twenties and dressed well," according to the clerk. Calderone likely didn't know any more than he put in the notes, but she wanted to ask him before she headed to Hy-Vee herself.

Back at her desk, she started a new to-do list. She wanted to revisit what they knew and try some new approaches.

- Ask out-of-town stores about bricks like the one thrown at my window (Mahan or Taylor)
- Ask local high school teachers and maybe Sweathog English teachers if they recognize handwriting on brick notes (Hammer and Taylor)
- Visit laundromat as a customer
- Visit Louella Belle's house
- Talk to store clerks about guy who didn't buy

Stopping by the laundromat and Louella Belle's house were her attempts to see if the two places would bring more to mind. She grinned. Her trunk held a throw-rug that was too big for her washer. She'd been meaning to take it to a different laundromat. Why not Squeaky's?

Calderone rapped on her office doorjamb. "Question, Chief?"

"Have a seat. Read what the grocery store clerks said. One thing jumped out at me."

"The guy who left without buying anything?"

"Exactly. I think the clerk thought he was good looking. Anything more than that?"

Calderone shook his head. "I asked. She was a nervous one. Maybe she'd give you a better description."

"Why do you think that?"

"I dunno. Isn't there some female code to describe who's a hunk?"

She rolled her eyes. "Maybe for teens. I'll stop by the store."

"The two clerks I talked to work like four to eight. After-school jobs."

"High school?" she asked.

"Yep. I know the girl's family a bit. Could be why she seemed nervous. Just young."

Calderone left and Elizabeth shrugged into her uniform parka. "Code indeed."

CHAPTER TWENTY

ON HER WAY OUT OF THE STATION late Friday morning, Elizabeth asked Hammer to think about who at the high school or college to ask about the handwriting. "Taylor might be able to help you out at the high school."

"We'll get on it, but with the schools closed, we may not get much right away.

She hadn't thought about that. "Oh, well. Do what you can."

Elizabeth drove her own car from the station to Squeaky Miller's businesses, and first went into the dry cleaners.

Squeaky had the morning paper spread on the counter and quickly closed it. "Morning, Chief. Just reading Jerry's article."

"Morning. Colorful, isn't it?" She had other words to describe the piece, but Squeaky would probably repeat them. "Wanted to let you know I'd be in the laundromat for an hour or so."

He frowned. "Following a new, whaddyacallit, lead?"

"No. I want to get a better sense of the place, so I brought a throw rug to wash."

Squeaky opened the drawer that she knew held laundry tickets and pens. ""Lemme give you some tokens."

Elizabeth held a hand at arm's length, palm facing him. "Nope. Not only am I on duty, but I need to wash the rug anyway."

He shut the drawer. "You won't, uh, turn on your lights or anything will you?"

She shook her head. "Brought my personal car."

"Good. Not too many people been using the place. Don't want anyone to think there's more bad stuff going on."

"Ah. When it's appropriate I'll mention that I've done laundry there since Louella Belle's murder. Let people know it's safe."

Squeaky shrugged. "Not sure much will help until you find her killer. But thanks."

Elizabeth went to her car's trunk and hauled out the multi-colored throw rug. Her cat often slept on it, so she shook it. A mix of brown and yellow cat hair fell to the snow."

She entered the laundromat and picked a machine close to the back of the business. From that vantage point, she'd see anyone who came in, and not everyone would notice her."

While the rug churned in a washer, she took in every inch of the laundromat. Louella Belle had been right about the lackluster cleaning job Squeaky did. If a broom had been handy she would have felt compelled to sweep out the corners.

She walked over to the laundry tub and stared into it. *I hope Louella Belle was gone before she was dunked in there.*

Next to the tub sat a commercial-sized, tan trash can with a black liner. It brimmed with lint, empty packages of laundry soap, dryer sheets, and food wrappers. She decided to do Squeaky a favor and remove the full bag. He probably had an empty one under it.

She lugged the trash bag from the container, pulled its draw string shut, and placed it by the back door. Then she peered into the bottom of the can. It held a couple of empty can liners, but also something that looked like a black pancake.

Elizabeth tilted the can so she could reach inside to pull out the liners and the flat object. She recognized the brown felt hat with its now-wrinkled feather. She held it with just her thumb and forefinger and placed it on the folding table where Louella Belle herself had lain a few short days ago.

Final Cycle

Elizabeth didn't routinely carry an evidence bag, but she always had a gallon-sized zippered bag. She took it from her coat pocket, opened it, and slid the hat into it pushing with only her thumbnail.

Felt wouldn't be a good source for prints, and Louella Belle's hat likely fell off her head rather than been taken off by her killer. Still, someone had put it in that can, maybe even deliberately placed it under the liner. And she had learned a lesson. Triple search every crime scene.

Elizabeth called Hammer. "I have a present for you." She relayed what she'd found and asked him to send someone over with a proper evidence bag.

"Damn, Chief. We missed it. I'm sorry."

"Key word is we. It's a fluke that I found it. We'll always know to check under the trash can liner from now on."

Calderone walked in ten minutes later, wearing an expression Elizabeth took to be guilt.

"Damn, Chief. We missed it."

"Did you rehearse that line with Hammer?" She smiled.

"No, but I feel terrible." He regarded the hat in its plastic bag. "I don't think she had a head wound, so no blood, right?"

"No. We can ask Skelly, but I think it's useless in terms of clues. But you never know, it may come in handy."

"Meaning what?" he asked.

"No idea. I would never have found it if Squeaky emptied his trash."

Calderone ogled her. "*You* emptied his trash?"

"Just for fun."

The bell above the laundromat door jingled and Squeaky came in. "I saw Calderone go in. Everything okay?"

Elizabeth and Calderone said, "Yes," and Elizabeth added, "I found Louella Belle's hat. Hadn't even realized it was missing."

Squeaky frowned. "I been in here a few times, didn't see it."

Elizabeth grinned. "Luckily you didn't empty your trash." She tilted her head toward the alley door. "I did."

Squeaky took in the large, full trash bag, and reddened. "I shouldn't let it get so full."

ELIZABETH ATE A SUB sandwich at her desk Friday and studied the hat that sat in front of her. "Why did someone put it in the trash rather than in the dryer with Louella Belle?"

Hammer's voice came from the hallway. "Talking to me, Chief?"

"Nope. Just myself."

"Fine as long as you don't expect an answer."

She groaned. "Smart-ass."

Hammer chuckled as he walked toward the break room.

She dialed Skelly.

"Logland Veterinary."

She laughed. "You are such a wise-acre."

"Cat okay?"

"She even ate hard food this morning."

"I don't think she had a jaw injury," he said.

"I know. She held out for soft food because I'd been giving it to her. Now she knows I won't coddle her."

Skelly's tone held humor. "Coddling never hurts, Elizabeth."

"I'll remember that if you break a leg. Listen, I have a business question."

He listened while she explained where she'd found the hat, and added, "Even if it held evidence, it's been in that barrel – or someplace – for days. An attorney would say any evidence on it was the height of meaningless."

"She had no wounds, so I wouldn't expect any of her blood. I can check it for any fluids. Felt wouldn't have usable prints."

"I'm not sure why, but I want to hang onto it for a day or two. Hey, did anyone claim Louella Belle's body?"

"Sadly, no family. Her attorney arranged for her to be sent to Leaving the Farm Funeral Home."

"Any services?"

"You'd have to ask John Stone," Skelly said.

"I might do that. Talk to you soon."

"Promises, promises," Skelly said.

Elizabeth flushed as she hung up. *Skelly and his insinuations.*

Final Cycle

EN ROUTE TO THE GROCERY store, Elizabeth drove around the Logland town square. Two days before Christmas, with the temperature at an almost-balmy thirty-three degrees, the middle of the square would usually host people looking at the decorated tree or kids throwing snowballs.

No one strode on the shoveled walkways. On top of wanting justice for the two victims, she resented that the person had stolen the town's Christmas joy.

Not a single child played in a yard along the drive to the Hy-Vee. Aloud, she said, "We've got to catch this killer."

In the grocery store, she found the manager. "We haven't seen any video from the night Stanley was killed. Is the store having problems getting it?"

"It's fine to share with police. I told your officer I'd look into it, and I called the regional office. They said our contract is with a local firm. They haven't called back."

"I bet I know who that is. They don't monitor in real time, do they?"

He shook his head. "They keep the digital files for a few weeks, and we can ask for them. Beyond that, I think they're gone."

"I'll have someone talk to them. I also wondered if the two clerks who were here that night are on duty."

He frowned. "I think you folks already talked to them."

"Officer Calderone did. Sometimes people remember more a couple days later."

"Kimberly's here. I'll have her meet you in the café."

After checking to see if she wanted one of her parents present – she didn't – Elizabeth and Kimberly sat in the deserted store café.

They nursed hot chocolate as Elizabeth broached her topic. "I'm sure it's hard to think about being one of the last people to see Mr. Buttons."

Kimberly nodded vigorously. "Alive, you mean."

"I know you talked to Officer Calderone. Sometimes we remember things a couple of days later that didn't initially occur to us. Our subconscious mind bugs us, so to speak. Can you think of more about that night?"

Kimberly frowned. "I think I told Tony everything." She flushed at Elizabeth's smile. "He knows my uncle, so we call him Tony."

"I would too, if he was my neighbor or something."

She nodded. "I've thought more about the guy who left the store a minute or two after Mr. Buttons."

Elizabeth tried to look encouraging as she sipped hot chocolate.

"He was kind of cute." She flushed. "But old. I mean, at least twenty-one or two."

"Old," Elizabeth said.

"He doesn't come in much, and he never says anything except hello or thank you."

"Tall, short?"

"Taller than you, but not as tall as Tony."

That left about eight inches of uncertainty, but Elizabeth didn't say so. "Thin or heavy?"

"Pretty thin. He had a dark-colored coat on that night. He usually dresses, well, pretty stylish."

Stylish was not a word Elizabeth often heard used to describe men. "You mean like the latest fashion?"

"I don't even know what's latest for men." Kimberly paused. "His jeans were ironed, and he had on what I think was an expensive sweater. Dark blue."

Bingo. Calderone had been right. Kimberly had more to say to another woman. "This is very helpful. Hair color?"

"Not blonde. Not red either. Kind of brownish. Not dark brown."

"Okay, Kimberly. If he comes in, I would like to talk to him. Maybe he saw something in the parking lot that would be helpful."

"Should I ask him to call you?"

"I was about to say definitely don't do that. If you can quietly give us a call when he comes in, fine. Or ask your manager to. If not, you don't need to tell or ask him anything. Just call us when he leaves." Elizabeth handed her a card with the station number on the front and her cell phone handwritten on the back. "Call me rather than 9-1-1, if you don't mind."

Kimberly took the card and her eyes brightened. "Am I like a junior detective?"

Elizabeth smiled. "I'm sure you'd be a good one, but please remember to simply call."

BACK AT HER DESK, Elizabeth buzzed Hammer. "Who has better contacts with the firm that does some of the local retail stores' security monitoring?"

"The place I know is called All Eyes on You, and the manager is usually pretty helpful. She grew up here."

"The Hy-Vee manager said she hasn't called back. He bet he didn't tell them it was important. Can you check it out? I want to know if Stanley Buttons interacted with a slim guy in ironed blue jeans right before he died."

"Who irons blue jeans?"

"Apparently this guy. Should make him easier to spot."

Five minutes later, Elizabeth took a call on her cell phone from an excited Wally. "On the online police report a few days ago, it said two more bikes had been taken. I think I found them."

Within ten minutes, Elizabeth and Calderone stood next to the middle school bike rack. It did indeed hold the two missing bicycles. Wheel tracks in the snow indicated they had recently been placed there.

Wally looked as excited as if he'd won the lottery. "Bet they were brought here last night."

"What makes you sat that?" Elizabeth asked.

He gestured behind him. "You can see this spot from the backs of those houses. During the day, someone would have seen anyone over here."

Calderone popped open the back of his pickup truck, which he'd brought to retrieve the bikes. "Good point. What even made you look here, Wally?"

"When I was eating my oatmeal today, I thought more about where they'd be. Cause I figured whoever took them mostly wanted to screw with you guys."

Elizabeth smiled. "I thought so, too."

Wally literally puffed out his chest. "I got to thinking if I did it, I'd hide 'em in the back of a shed or in plain sight. So I started looking at bike racks around town."

"I'm impressed," Elizabeth said.

Calderone put on gloves so he could lift the bikes into his truck. He gave Wally an exaggerated wink. "Heard you're coming by the station Christmas Eve. Hammer spikes the punch."

CHAPTER TWENTY-ONE

FINDING THE BIKES HAD been a boost but, as Elizabeth expected, they'd been wiped clean of prints. She told Calderone and Hammer to go ahead and call the families who reported them stolen so they could pick them up. At least one crime would be solved by Christmas.

She decided to cross one more item off her Friday to-do list. She firmly believed that talking to a victim or assailant in their home environment could explain a lot about them. Absent that in Louella Belle's case, her home could offer more traces of her life and maybe which aspect of it led to her death.

Officers had done a cursory search of the house soon after the murder. Because she wasn't looking for anything to incriminate Louella Belle in a crime, the state's attorney for the county said Elizabeth could go through her belongings without a warrant indicating what else police expected to find.

She called Louella Belle's lawyer, John Stone and said she'd like to stop by Louella Belle's former home after work.

"My only caution is not to remove anything without talking to me first. I've hired someone to do an inventory of her things."

"I won't. My officers have been in her house, but I haven't. Does someone inherit her home and possessions?"

Stone spoke quickly. "She had her will with me, but left no instructions for any material items."

Elizabeth didn't tell him that was a pretty good non-answer.

She drove to Louella Belle's neighborhood and parked her small Ford two doors down from Louella Belle's place, not wanting to attract neighbors' attention. Sidewalks had been cleared, but Christmas Eve was forecast to bring more snow. South-Central Illinois seemed to be on a path for fifty total inches of snow this season, a lot compared to the past few years.

She used the key John Stone provided and walked into the house. Someone had turned the heat fairly low, and cool, stuffy air enveloped her.

The bungalow's interior proved to be more spacious than its exterior implied. The living/dining room combo was easily twenty five feet long, and fifteen feet wide. Sofa and chairs were a severe dark blue, and end tables held only lamps, no books or needlework. The only extraneous item was a narrow, open box that held a fountain pen. It sat on a small table next to the phone.

Elizabeth crossed the room's width and entered a broad hallway. On the left was the kitchen, and immediately across the hall, the bathroom. To the right, the hall ended with two bedrooms that faced each other.

Between the bedrooms, a narrow staircase provided access to a second floor, which from the outside appeared to be more of a dormer than third bedroom.

Elizabeth stood in the doorway to the most lived-in looking room, Louella Belle's bedroom. "Heck of a way to spend the Friday before Christmas."

She moved to the almost six-foot-long closet that faced the bed and slid open the door. The metal door track squeaked in protest.

The clothes were organized by color, and Louella Belle had fewer than a lot of women her age. Some older women, including Elizabeth's mother, kept clothes they no longer wore. They could hold sentimental value. Others were a smaller size than they now used – but maybe hoped to wear again.

Generally, Louella Belle had dressed in neutral or dark colors. Elizabeth had never seen her in spring pastels or gay holiday sweatshirts.

Hangers at the far left of the closet bore two outfits with a few wrinkles, maybe items she had recently worn and intended to wear again before washing them. Elizabeth felt in the pockets of two pairs of pants and found nothing, but a brown herringbone jacket provided several pieces of paper.

Before she finished unfolding the first one, Elizabeth recognized it as the half-page flyer with the two Maxwell children. She reread the text about poisoning kids with food, then squinted to read small print Louella Belle had added under the photo, in red pen. "Dead before forty."

"Gee, Louella Belle. That's harsh."

A smaller piece turned out to be a white three-by-five card folded in half. It had the name of Donald Dingle, a phone number Elizabeth recognized as city hall, and one additional word. *Laundromat.*

"Damn that man!" She now felt certain that Louella Belle wouldn't have been in the laundromat if Dingle hadn't told her to keep an eye out for students loitering there – or whatever he had told her. Had she not gone into the laundromat, she would be alive.

Did she anger her killer by demanding information about what they were doing, or did an evil person simply walk into the place looking for someone to kill? The latter seemed less likely, but some people were unhappy close to Christmas and took it out on innocent folks.

Furious, Elizabeth replaced the paper in the jacket pocket. She then took out her own notebook and jotted a note to tell John Stone she would like to keep the card that referred to Donald Dingle.

Ten minutes later, the bedroom had yielded nothing unexpected for an older, retired woman. The absence of almost all personal effects bothered Elizabeth– no photos, letters, mementos, or even decorative bric-a-brac.

The second bedroom made up for the almost Spartan condition of the room in which Louella Belle had slept. Along one wall were pictures of the family of her youth. While a few included parents, most were a young Louella Belle with a girl perhaps two years younger than she. The resemblance was so strong Elizabeth thought she had to be a sister, maybe a cousin, but sister made more sense.

Photos of a smiling Louella Belle seemed to indicate she had not always been a sour prognosticator. But when Louella

Belle was about twelve, the photos stopped, save one. In that one, Louella Belle stood between her parents, each somber, all in dark clothing. The mother's black dress could have been that of a Puritan in the seventeenth century, just slightly shorter.

Elizabeth felt certain the three Simpsons had attended the funeral of the other child. "How awful," she whispered.

Nothing on the walls indicated how the little girl died. Feeling like an intruder at a wake, Elizabeth opened two of the four built-in cabinets under maple bookshelves. The detritus of a child's short life stared at her -- small stuffed animals, a toy wooden caboose, children's books, and what looked to be a scrapbook.

She hesitated for only a few seconds before pulling out the scrapbook. What could it possibly tell her about Louella Belle's adult life? Elizabeth would suggest that John Stone remove the photos and scrapbook before a firm arrived to inventory the contents of the house. These items should not end up in an estate auction.

She sat in a rocking chair, album on her lap, and began thumbing through it. The first two pages held only photos of Louella Belle with her parents, plus an older woman Elizabeth assumed was a grandmother.

When Louella Belle was about two, the second daughter arrived. "Our new Bundle of Joy," read the first caption of mother, newborn, and a rapt Louella Belle. She looked at her little sister with an adoring expression.

Soon, the expressions reversed. The sibling, Deanna Dawn, reserved her most radiant smiles for her big sister. Photos included birthday parties, lots of snow people, and a bunch of first (and last) days of school. Several showed the girls in a large vegetable garden, pointing to huge pumpkins and watermelons.

And then the obituary for Deana Dawn Simpson, who died of anaphylactic shock after eating shellfish. In flowery language, the article listed her favorite color (yellow) and happiest time of her life (a trip the prior year to Disneyland). Parents and sister Louella Belle were described as devastated.

Aloud, Elizabeth said, "And there it is. Food as poison."

Only when she spoke did Elizabeth become aware of her stuffy nose and the tears rolling down her cheeks. Louella Belle had been wracked with pain, but the only way she could assuage it seemed to be to cause some for others.

A noise near the back door made Elizabeth sit up straight and gently place the scrapbook on one of the shelves. She should have heard the person walk up the steps on the back porch.

No lights were on in the house. Dusk had fallen, and Elizabeth had been so engrossed she hadn't noticed.

The back door handle jiggled, and someone scraped metal on metal. Perhaps a key in a lock. No, Elizabeth thought, a key would mean a click and entry. She lowered herself to the floor and crawled to the door that led to the hallway.

After several seconds of metallic sounds, something crunched on the back doorframe. The likely burglar had apparently succeeded in wedging a screwdriver or something similar into the lock or doorframe, and was about to enter.

As the door pushed open, she unsnapped her holster, confident that the burglar's entry would hide most sounds she made. She drew her gun from its holster and undid the safety. It had a round in its chamber, but she hoped not to fire a shot.

A nearby streetlamp provided just enough light for Elizabeth to see a man's shape move through the kitchen, opening drawers and cabinets. He worked quickly, likely looking for cash or items easily pawned.

Logland had relatively few burglaries, and thieves who'd been interrupted generally had only their burglary tools. She reasoned tools could include a knife, but most burglars weren't looking for a fight. The plan was always to get in and out quickly without meeting a resident.

When Finn Clancy moved from the kitchen into the hallway en route to the living room, Elizabeth considered identifying herself. She held back. If he had killed Louella Belle, maybe whatever he sought would help prove it.

Clancy picked up the fountain pen in its box, snapped it shut, and stuffed it in a pants pocket. Then he turned to head toward the bedrooms. As he started toward them, Elizabeth stepped into the hallway, holding her gun at her side.

"Fancy seeing you here, Mr. Clancy."

He stood still, then grinned. "Guess we both had the same idea, Chief."

"And what would that be?"

"You know," he wet his lips, "checkin' on Louella Belle's house."

Elizabeth took one step closer to him. "Do you have a firearm or any other weapon with you?"

Clancy spread his hands and shrugged at the same time. "Chief. You know me."

"I do." Elizabeth raised her gun a few inches. "Do you have any weapons on you?"

Clancy's shoulders sagged. "No."

"Face the wall, put your hands above your shoulders and on the wall, and spread your feet well apart."

Clancy complied. "Jeez. Can't we settle this without all this formal stuff?"

"Stay facing the wall." Elizabeth took her cell from her pocket and pushed the emergency call option. When the 9-1-1 dispatcher responded, she said, "This is Chief Elizabeth Friedman in Logland. Transfer this call to my station, please. We have a ten-sixty-two in progress at the home of the late Louella Belle Simpson."

After telling the dispatcher that neither she or the B&E suspect had any injuries, Elizabeth hung up and studied Clancy's profile. "What did you think you'd find?"

Despite having had a couple of minutes to rehearse a response, Clancy had no good one. "I, uh, well, you know. It's almost Christmas."

"Wanted something to pawn to finish your shopping?" Elizabeth asked.

Clancy turned his head. "Do I get to keep the new bike?"

"My guess is you'll need a place to store it while you're a guest of the county or state."

"Hey! I…"

"Face the wall," Elizabeth said.

He complied. "I didn't kill Louella Belle."

Flashing red and blue lights announced back-up.

"You have a funny way of trying to convince me of that. Stay where you are while I open the door for my men."

"I'm gettin' a cramp in my leg."

Elizabeth opened the front door. "Suck it up."

CHAPTER TWENTY-TWO

THE SPACE ADJACENT TO the cement block room that held the station's two small cells served as an informal interrogation-room. A sparse room kept uncomfortable on purpose.

On television shows, police wanted to keep suspects on edge. Elizabeth didn't necessarily want to frighten people, but she wanted them to know they hadn't been brought in for a chat. Especially in this case, she wasn't about to use the more comfortable conference room.

With Calderone sitting next to her, Elizabeth started the questioning. "Had you broken into Louella Belle's house before?"

Clancy blew out a breath. "No, and I wouldn't have…"

"I'm going to ask you some specific questions," Elizabeth said. "Where were you before you got to Louella Belle's place?"

"Library."

"The library," Calderone said. "Taking out a book."

Clancy glowered at him. "They let you sit in there when it's cold outside."

"What were you going to do with anything you took from her house? Be hard to pawn locally."

Clancy looked from Elizabeth to Calderone and then at the table. "EBay."

Trying to keep sarcasm from her tone, Elizabeth asked, "Don't you get paid faster if you sell on Craig's List?"

"Yeah, but somebody might figure out where I got the stuff. You know, later. If it was in the papers."

After questioning Clancy for more than an hour, Elizabeth didn't see him as Louella Belle's killer. His earlier alibi still held, and she could think of no motive.

Sure, Louella Belle could have insulted him in the laundromat – or yelled at him if she found him in his underwear. But Clancy seemed to tune out insults, and Elizabeth thought he was more likely to have mooned Louella Belle than shove her hard enough to kill her.

Still, he was a logical enough suspect that she had no intention of letting him immediately bond out on the burglary attempt. Not that the decision was hers, but local judges tended to agree with her about who was a danger to themselves or others, or might skip out on bail.

Her eyes swept his untucked shirt and the hole in his jeans, but also took note of his clean and carefully cut fingernails. He no longer had family ties to the town, as far as she knew, and his address was a post office box. He seemed to be homeless. Yet he never appeared dirty. Where did he hang out?

Elizabeth stood from her position across the table from Clancy. "Officer Calderone and I are going to step out. You'll be on camera. Don't make me chain you to that chair."

Clancy replied in a sullen tone. "Yes ma'am."

She and Calderone left the room and shut the door. Elizabeth gestured to Grayson who'd been leaning against the wall a few yards down. "He's on the closed-circuit feed into the conference room, and Mahan's in the bullpen. Stand by the door to listen. If Clancy starts throwing a chair or something, holler for us."

Grayson nodded. "You think he killed her?"

"Or Stanley Buttons?" Calderone asked.

"He mostly sticks to his story, but every now and then he forgets something or repeats himself. If he did it, he's doing a good job of acting like an innocent man."

"What do you mean?" Grayson asked.

Elizabeth shrugged. "If he did it, I think his story would stay exactly the same. Easier for a made-up story to be consistent."

She nodded to Grayson and she and Calderone continued to the locker room, where Hammer had placed a fresh pot of coffee and a few sandwiches that Nick had sent from the diner.

In silence they poured their cups and unwrapped the food. As they sat, Elizabeth asked, "You think he'd tell us any more if we threaten to transfer him to county?"

"Might. Clancy's a creature of habit. Almost OCD-ish. He's expecting to be cut loose."

"I looked at his record. We've arrested him a few times, but I don't recall him ever starting the fights he was in."

Calderone swallowed a bite of sandwich. "The one time he threw the first punch, the guy he hit had called him a vile name and accused him of robbing somebody in the parking lot at the hospital."

"And did he? Rob someone?"

"Nope. Charges for the fight were dropped. I think the guy he hit was drunk and knew the robbery victim. Just mouthing off. Dangerous to do."

Elizabeth added sugar to her coffee. "I need to start keeping bottles of tea in here. I don't want this stuff after about three. So, you think if I threaten him with transfer to the county he'll be more, shall we say, forthcoming?"

"Could be. If he knows anything besides what he planned to take from Louella Belle's."

Elizabeth wrapped up half of her sandwich and grinned at Calderone. "Watch this."

They left the locker room, and Grayson's eyes lit up as they approached him.

"More sandwiches in the locker room. Help yourself."

"Yes ma'am." He glanced at Calderone as he walked by them.

Elizabeth figured Grayson thought the sandwich was too good for Clancy. She unlocked the door to the interrogation room and she and Calderone reentered.

Clancy glanced at the sandwich. "That for me?"

"Yes." She sat it in front of him. "You'll have missed dinner at the county lock-up, and I hear breakfast is cold cereal."

"County? I didn't do nothin'!" When he met Elizabeth's gaze, he added, "Well, I was gonna take something, but I didn't, did I?"

She and Calderone sat across from Clancy again. "You know something about Louella Belle. Maybe you didn't kill her, but you've been too close to this murder all along. Your bike was nearby, you're in that laundromat regularly, and now you've broken into her house. A dead woman's house."

Clancy unwrapped the ham half-sandwich and took a huge bite. With his mouth full, he said, "Thank you."

Calderone said, "Like the chief said, last good meal you'll get for a while."

Clancy's eye's traveled from one to the other. "I don't want to go to county. Hell, I'd be there for freaking Christmas, too."

He paused, and Elizabeth thought it was more for effect.

"I didn't kill her, but I might know who did."

Elizabeth and Calderone said nothing as he took another bite.

Clancy added, "So do I go to jail if I didn't tell you something, you know, first time you asked?"

Elizabeth wiggled her hand, palm down, above the table. "Maybe, maybe not. If you help us catch a killer, that would weigh heavily in your favor." She turned to Calderone. "I think we ought to offer Mr. Clancy a lawyer again, what do you think?"

"Yep. You want one?"

Clancy seemed to stare at something over Elizabeth's shoulder, and then at her. "Do I get more credit if I talk to you without one?"

She shook her head. "No. You have every right to protect yourself. I can call the public defender for you."

"Yeah, I guess. Can I sleep here tonight?"

Bingo. Finn Clancy really didn't want to go to the county jail.

Calderone put Clancy in a cell and got him a blanket while Elizabeth went to her office to call the county Office of the Public Defender. She knew they wouldn't want to come out so late on such a cold night, when the death hadn't taken place that night. Too bad.

AT ALMOST MIDNIGHT FRIDAY NIGHT, the young public defender finished talking to Clancy in the conference room and called for Elizabeth and Calderone.

As they sat, Max Henderson adjusted reading glasses and peered at scribbled notes on a legal pad. Early balding made him appear older than what Elizabeth assumed was twenty-seven or eight. She'd looked him up on the Office of Public Defender website. University of Illinois Law School, and a native of the state.

"Chief, Officer, I think my client can help you a lot. He agrees he should have done so earlier." Henderson nodded to Clancy, who ducked his head, seeming to try to adopt a self-effacing pose.

Elizabeth thought he failed miserably. "Glad to see he's had a change of heart."

Henderson continued. "He is willing to speak without an agreement on reduced likelihood of arrest, to give you a sense of what he knows."

"I'm not the State's Attorney's Office for the county, Mr. Henderson. If you want a representative of that office here, I can make a call. I simply want to know what Mr. Clancy knows that would help us arrest a killer. Assuming he's helpful I'll urge full consideration as they contemplate his tardiness in coming forward."

Calderone briefly looked amused, but then the expression passed. Elizabeth raised an eyebrow at Henderson as he pondered what she had said.

Henderson turned to Clancy and nodded. "Keep it to what we discussed."

Clancy sat up straighter, and squared his shoulders. "It was the two fat dudes. The ones from the college."

CHAPTER TWENTY-THREE

AS TIRED AS SHE KNEW everyone was, Elizabeth wanted to push through the early hours of Saturday morning. She could not imagine two less likely suspects for Louella Belle's murder than Herbie Hiccup and Just Juice Jenson. But the implausible nature of Clancy's accusation gave it a ring of truth. If Clancy had a manufactured tale, he would have picked a better one.

"Let's say we want to believe you…" Elizabeth began.

Clancy half-stood. "You asked me to tell you!"

Lawyer Henderson put a hand on Clancy's forearm and forced him back into his chair. "I told you. Listen and answer questions. That's it."

Clancy sat. "I didn't kill that mouthy broad."

Henderson blanched.

Elizabeth said, "So far, I believe you. Now tell me why you think Mr. Gibson and Mr. Jenson killed Louella Belle Simpson."

"I saw 'em less than a minute after."

"Where was that?" Calderone asked.

Clancy stared at him for a couple of seconds. "I come in the back door of Squeaky's laundry place. They were in the back, in front of that tub where you can wash stuff by hand."

"Was Louella Belle alive?" Elizabeth asked. "Standing? Lying on the floor?"

Final Cycle

"On her back, on the floor. Her head was crooked. Her neck, I guess."

Without looking at the pad in front of her, Elizabeth wrote 'crooked.' "Where were Gibson and Jenson? Did someone check for a pulse?"

Clancy nodded. "They was kneeling next to her, Gibson on the left, I think. Looked like a couple of stupid ducks after their babies fell into a sewer grate. Kinda wavin' hands. One of 'em kept saying 'what'll we do? what'll we do?'"

"And what did you do?" Elizabeth asked.

"I pushed Gibson away from her. Heavy bastard. Didn't feel no pulse in her neck."

"Did you think about calling 9-1-1?" Calderone asked.

Elizabeth recognized the sarcasm in his question.

Clancy glanced sideways at his lawyer. "I probably shoulda. But, I, uh, saw an opportunity to make some money."

Henderson stopped taking notes on his legal pad and shut his eyes for a half-second.

"And what opportunity was that?" Elizabeth asked.

"See, I owe some money down at the pool hall, where I hang out a lot."

Elizabeth waited, expecting him to say he rifled Louella Belle's pockets.

Clancy continued. "I told the fat boys I could help make it so no one knew they had anything to do with her killin'."

Calderone asked, "How did you plan to do that?"

He grinned briefly. "I figure, we hide her and leave. First I thought in that huge tan garbage can in the back, near the laundry tub thing. Then I had the idea of the dryer."

"Did you all lift Louella Belle into the dryer?" Elizabeth asked.

"Mostly me and the Juice guy. We put her on top of one of those carts and kinda rolled her over to the dryer. One with somethin' in it, so we could kinda hide her."

"And no one came in while you did this?" Calderone asked.

Clancy hesitated for a fraction of a second. "Nope. We worked pretty fast. Put her in the dryer with the red and white tablecloth things. Where Marti found her."

Elizabeth picked up her now cold cup of coffee. "And why was hiding the body of an elderly woman an 'opportunity' for you?"

"Oh, I told 'em they had to give me $500. See, I could pay off some guys."

"At the pool hall," Calderone said.

Clancy nodded, seeming to take Calderone's casual tone as agreement that hiding a body was a good way to make quick money.

"Couple more questions," Elizabeth said. "How did Louella Belle's head and upper torso get wet?"

Clancy wet his lips. "See, uh." He glanced at his lawyer.

Elizabeth figured the next couple sentences would be news to Henderson.

When Clancy said nothing, Calderone asked, "Did she get dirty on the floor?"

Clancy's temper flared. "We wanted to be sure she was dead. Dunked her head in the laundry tub."

Henderson interjected, "Now Chief, we planned on some limits to the disclosures here."

Elizabeth waved his comment aside. "If Mr. Clancy is to describe Louella Belle's death. I think the dunk in the laundry tub is quite relevant."

For the first time, Clancy seemed to realize he had implicated himself in more than disposing of a body. He almost stuttered. "But she, she, musta been dead. I mean, she didn't wake up. That's what we were trying to do. Wake her, wake her up."

Elizabeth didn't acknowledge his supposed good deed. "So, she was wet when you transported her to the dryer. All three of you wedged her in there?"

Clancy nodded.

"Who cleaned up the wet floor?" Calderone asked.

"Dunno. I left. I told 'em to give me the money the next day. Met 'em at the Weed 'n Feed."

"What time?" Elizabeth asked.

"Dunno. Kinda lunchtime. They said they needed to get the cash in the morning."

"Did they say where it would come from?" Calderone asked.

"Like I give a flying...I didn't care. Long as it was green bills."

"Did you leave the laundromat together?" Elizabeth asked?

"Nope. I walked right out the back door. No idea what the fatsos did."

"How did your bike get behind Gene's place?"

Clancy shrugged. "How the hell would I know?"

Though she figured Clancy had left it there himself and gone to Dollar General or the Weed 'n Feed – which Mahan had verified – she decided to leave the bike for another round of questioning.

"Funny someone took it from the bike rack in front of Doris Minx' place and left it there," Calderone said.

"Funny, yeah," Clancy said.

Henderson cleared his throat. "I believe my client has been very helpful to you."

Elizabeth nodded. "We learned a lot." She focused on Clancy. "However, you were more involved in Louella Belle's death than you indicated."

"I still get out of here though, right?" Clancy asked.

"Bond is up to the court, but I imagine that at some point you will be free until trial."

Clancy leaned forward, toward Elizabeth. "Whaddya mean trial?"

"Earlier, I had the sense you only witnessed something. You were an active participant in moving a body, and took money to stay quiet about that." Elizabeth didn't use the term 'accessory after the fact.'

"We had a deal," Clancy began.

"You helped us," Elizabeth said. "Possibly a lot. I will make sure the Office of the State's Attorney knows that."

"I don't want to spend effing Christmas in jail!"

Elizabeth stared Clancy down. "We'll see about that."

AS CALDERONE AND GRAYSON took Clancy back to a cell at two AM, Elizabeth stayed in the conference room with Max Henderson. "My guess is some of that was new to you."

In a stiff tone, he said, "I can't comment about what my client and I discussed."

She smiled. "It was more of a rhetorical statement, based on your expression a couple of times."

Henderson said nothing.

"When you review Mr. Clancy's past crimes, you'll see they generally didn't involve hurting anyone. I will tell the State's Attorney that he was helpful. If they ask me about bail, I can't be as fulsome in my support of it as I was before I knew he dunked her in that tub."

Henderson put his legal pad and pen in a cardboard accordion folder. "I hear you." He hesitated. "Thanks for your attitude." He left.

Elizabeth pondered her so-called attitude for a few moments. As with giving Clancy the sandwich earlier, she thought she got more from basic courtesy than insults. Keeping derision from her tone had been hard, though.

Calderone and Grayson came back into the conference room, Calderone covering a yawn with the back of his hand.

Elizabeth gestured to chairs across the table from her. "You can go home in a few, Calderone."

Grayson asked, "What do you want me to do, Chief?"

"Since we have Clancy in a cell, I want you to stay in the station instead of going back out. Most students are home so bars closed early, and it's bone-chilling cold. Any thief checking for change in unlocked cars deserves to find some."

Calderone yawned again. "Sorry."

"No problem. You go home, I'm going to nap in my office for a couple hours, then get Gibson and Jenson in here pretty early."

"You really think they did it?" Grayson asked.

Elizabeth shrugged. "Had to be more than Clancy moving poor Louella Belle around the laundromat. I want to question them. My guess is they'll be so close to wetting themselves that we'll get answers pretty quickly."

CHAPTER TWENTY-FOUR

AT SIX AM SATURDAY, Elizabeth splashed water on her face in the station restroom and combed her hair. She hadn't napped in her uniform jacket, so it bolstered her appearance as much as fresh lipstick.

She headed to the break room to make the first pot of coffee, then snooped around Hammer's desk for donut leftovers from Friday. She found none, so she ate an emergency granola bar from her locker.

Elizabeth finalized her notes on the conversation with Clancy and his lawyer. A few minutes before seven, the station's back door opened and someone stomped feet on the mat to shake off the slush that had refrozen overnight.

"That you Hammer?"

"Hey Chief. Need something?"

"Come on back after you get coffee. No big rush."

She could hear him talk to someone and realized it was Grayson. Of course. She'd told him to stay in the station.

Food smells drifted down the hall. Hammer had brought breakfast sandwiches for them, including Clancy. She got up from behind her desk and followed the smells.

In the locker room, a bleary-eyed Grayson sat on a bench as Hammer stowed his coat in a locker. "Morning guys."

"Chief," they both said.

"Grayson, you in one piece?"

"Yeah. Clancy's snores would wake the dead and they'll be in my head all day when I sleep."

"I caught three hours." She nodded at the two bags of fast food and then looked at Hammer. "Make sure you get reimbursed."

"I will. You want me to take his food to him?"

"Is he still sleeping, Grayson?"

"Unless he just woke up. He hollered for me about four and I took him to the john."

"He doesn't want to go to county, but if he doesn't bail out today we may have to do that. We aren't set up for escorting inmates and feeding three squares."

Hammer shut his locker. "Agreed." He looked at Grayson. "If the Chief says you can head home, I'll take him food in an hour. Or earlier if he calls out."

Elizabeth took a sandwich from the bag. "Beats the granola bar I had in my locker. Head home, Grayson. Thanks for pulling guard duty."

He snorted. "My tailbone did not like that hard chair."

She didn't respond. Grayson had been known to nap in his patrol car. Maybe she should put a hard seat in it.

Hammer picked up the bags of food, offered a sandwich to Grayson, who did not take one, and turned toward Elizabeth. "Calderone sent me a text I just read. You want me to get those two Sweathog guys down here?"

Elizabeth walked into the hall with him. "When Mahan comes in. I told Calderone to sleep a couple extra hours. Come to my office with Mahan and we'll strategize."

"Oh boy," Hammer said. "Is that Chicago police talk?"

"Up there we would say, 'Let's meet and get this the hell over with.'"

"Works down here," Hammer said.

WHEN NEITHER HERBIE OR Just Juice answered Hammer's calls, Elizabeth told Mahan she'd ride to their apartment complex with him to strongly suggest the men drive to the station. "If they're sleeping, they can crash again when we're done. Either at their place or here, as our guests."

The two men lived across the hall from each other in an older, red brick, college-owned apartment building. Elizabeth had not been in them, but had heard all units were efficiencies and up to three students could live in each apartment. Sounded crowded to her, but probably roomier than a three-person dorm room.

The early morning Saturday drive through town felt peaceful. Christmas season usually did, though Elizabeth thought this year was shaping up to be a very different holiday.

As they pulled up in front of the building, an older, possibly dark blue, Ford SUV pulled out of the parking lot at the side of the building. Snow spatter covered both sides, and the rest of the SUV looked as if it had not been washed in months.

Behind the wheel sat Herbie Hiccup, with Just Juice Jenson in the passenger seat. A quick glance showed the SUV was loaded to the roof with boxes and suitcases

"Would you say the guys are going on a trip?" Mahan asked.

"Taking us for a ride, I'd say." Elizabeth tapped the car's internal dome light. "Turn on your pretty red and blue ones. No need for a siren."

"With pleasure." Mahan flipped the switch that set the bubble atop the car in rotation.

Though they were less than two car lengths behind the duo, the SUV continued down College Avenue, heading west.

"What do they think they're doing?" Mahan asked.

Elizabeth half-laughed. "Their version of a getaway, I suppose."

"But what's the point?"

Elizabeth thought for a moment. "I bet they figure we won't follow them outside of town."

"Amazing these whack-a-doodles made it out of high school." Mahan honked the police car's horn.

Elizabeth dialed 9-1-1 and told the county dispatcher they would follow the SUV onto county roads, and gave its license number.

The woman asked, "Need any help, Chief Friedman?"

"No, just a couple of dumb guys who figure we turn our car around at the town's edge. Thanks, though."

As city streets turned into rural roads that traveled beside now-harvested corn fields, Mahan honked the car horn in rapid succession. "They can't say they didn't hear us."

"Get on their tail," Elizabeth said.

Mahan edged closer until only about ten feet separated the police car and SUV. After ten seconds, the SUV's brake lights began coming off and on. Mahan pulled back as the SUV slowed.

"Give them a few more seconds," Elizabeth said. "If they don't stop, turn on the siren."

Within five seconds, the van began to edge to the side of the road and slowed.

"No shoulder here," Mahan said.

As they stopped, Elizabeth opened the passenger door. "Hang here for a minutes. I'm going to tell them to turn around and we'll follow them to the station."

She unholstered her gun and held it at her side. The SUV's driver's window came down and a chubby hand held out a driver's license. And then dropped it.

"Out of the car," Elizabeth said.

The driver's door opened first, and Herbie almost slid out. "Um. Hello Chief Friedman. Can we help you?"

The passenger door opened and Elizabeth could hear Just Juice's ample form land on the snow-covered brown grass that ran along the road. "Come around here, Mr. Jenson. Walk in front of your vehicle, please."

Elizabeth studied them. Both wore lightweight jackets, having expected to be in the SUV rather than standing in the cold. They wore expressions similar to a kid who took chocolate from a sibling's Christmas stocking. Neither appeared armed.

She replaced her gun in its holster. "Where were you guys going?"

They spoke simultaneously. "Home."

"Finished your studying?"

Neither responded.

"We have some questions for you. I want you to turn around and Officer Mahan and I will follow you back to the police station."

Final Cycle

"We're kinda late," Herbie said.

"Or we can stand out here in the cold while we have Officer Calderone join us. Then I can put you in separate police cars for the ride. Handcuffed of course."

Just Juice's shoulders sagged and Herbie said, "I'll drive."

AT THE STATION, Elizabeth put the two men in the conference room. She didn't specifically want to give them better treatment than Clancy. She didn't want the two to know Clancy resided down the hall. Or vice-versa.

To herself, she repeated, "Herbert Gibson and Erasmus Jenson." She didn't want to slip up and call them Herbie Hiccup or Just Juice. Not out loud, anyway.

"So, gentlemen, we have a lot to discuss this Saturday morning. Let's start with why you decided to leave town when you said you planned to stay here over Christmas to study."

"Do we need a lawyer?" Herbie asked.

"As I said when we arrived at the station, you have a right to counsel."

Just Juice cleared his throat. "Like we said, we haven't done anything wrong." He looked at Herbie. "We'd have to pay for a lawyer."

Elizabeth tapped her pen on her notebook. "Also as I said earlier, if you can't afford a lawyer, one will be provided."

Calderone spoke up. "But you need to decide either way, so we can get this show on the road."

Before either man responded, someone knocked lightly on the conference room door. Hammer entered and handed a note to Elizabeth.

She read it silently. *Clancy's lawyer arranged a bail hearing at ten. Judge wants you there.*

Elizabeth tilted the note so Calderone could see it. She kept her face expressionless as she handed the note back to Hammer. "Tell him I'll be there."

She turned to Herbie and Just Juice. "Gentlemen, I have to be in court in forty-five minutes on another case. Won't be long. We'll talk for a few minutes now and resume when I return."

In a bolder tone than he had previously used, Jenson said, "Chief, we need to get our own show on the road. Can't this wait until after the holidays?"

"You must think I just fell off the proverbial turnip truck." Elizabeth paused for several seconds. She had planned to dive into Louella Belle's case, but didn't want to stop and start over. It would give Just Juice and Herbie too much time to think.

"Why were you leaving town?" Elizabeth asked.

The two men looked at each other and Herbie spoke. "We heard you picked up Finn Clancy and thought he might tell you lies about us."

Elizabeth held his gaze. "Had you come to see me to dispute a lie, rather than trying to leave town, I'd be more likely to see your perspective."

Just Juice glowered at Herbie. "I told you we should come here!"

Good, let them start to argue with each other.

Calderone asked, "How did you know we picked up Clancy?"

"It's all over town. We heard at the sub shop near the highway, about ten last night."

She asked, "What lies might Mr. Clancy have told us?"

Herbie said, "I guess we do need a lawyer."

Elizabeth stood and Calderone followed suit. "I'll send Sergeant Hammer in to make arrangements. If you leave this room without permission, I'll handcuff you to those chairs." She shut the door with a firm bang.

Calderone looked at her. "Turnip truck? Not exactly Chicago talk."

She grinned. "I heard Mahan say it once."

CHAPTER TWENTY-FIVE

ELIZABETH DEBATED TAKING Calderone or Mahan to the bail hearing. But she decided she wanted more officers than usual in the station, even though Clancy would be at the hearing with his attorney.

The county courthouse was on the town square, only two blocks from the police station, and Elizabeth wanted some cold air to wake her up. She strode briskly down a mix of shoveled and unshoveled sidewalks. She returned a few greetings, but minus her official hat and in a heavy parka, most people didn't recognize her.

She greeted the sole guard who staffed the magnetometer in the courthouse lobby. He didn't look happy to see her on a Saturday – much less a Saturday two days before Christmas.

Elizabeth slid into the seat behind the county state's attorney just as the door to Judge Kemper's chamber opened. Donaldson, one of the more self-centered people in town, turned briefly to her. "Nice you could make it, Chief."

Stuffed shirt. "You've probably heard we have a lot going on."

The bailiff called, "All rise."

Judge Kemper was so tall he had to stoop to walk through a couple doorways in the old courthouse. A quick glance told Elizabeth his robes should be a couple inches longer. He reached his elevated bench, knocked lightly with his gavel, and looked at Donaldson. "Tell me why we're having a bail hearing two days before Christmas for a man who broke into the home of a recent murder victim."

Donaldson stood and launched into an explanation about Clancy not being a suspect in Louella Belle's murder. He added that Chief Friedman indicated she did not oppose bail because Clancy had provided useful information in the case.

"That true, Chief Friedman?" Kemper asked.

"Yes sir." When the judge made a gimme gesture, she added, "I'd rather not state what the assistance was in open court. Would you like me to approach the bench?"

He waved a hand. "For now, if you two agree that's good enough for me to start the hearing." He turned to Max Henderson, who sat next to Clancy. "Tell me why your client will be no danger to anyone and will stay in town."

Henderson acknowledged Clancy's nonviolent run-ins with police and stressed his recent willing assistance to law enforcement. "Beyond that, Your Honor, Mr. Clancy is not a man of means. He has support systems in place in Logland that he could not duplicate elsewhere."

"And where will Mr. Clancy reside while he is on bail?"

Henderson had a ready answer. "I have spoken with folks at the Logland Mission, which is near the Salvation Army store."

"I know where it is, counselor," the judge said.

"Yes, sir. Mr. Clancy has stayed there many times, and is never a problem to others who use the facility. As long as he is in the Mission when it opens at seven PM and leaves when it closes for the day at seven AM, he's welcome there."

The judge faced Clancy. "And how will you wile away the daytime hours?"

"I hang out at the library a lot. Folks at McDonald's don't mind if I spend an hour or two there for meals."

Judge Kemper peered at Clancy over his bifocals. "I'd like some collateral."

"I don't have much money, Your Honor, just from SSI."

"Supplemental Security Income," the judge said.

Elizabeth thought he was about to ask something, but changed his mind. Her own question about Clancy's income source had been answered. SSI was for people on disability who hadn't worked enough to collect Social Security Disability. She'd try to find out the basis for him getting it, but figured he had some form of documented depression. Or at least convinced Social Security he was depressed rather than lazy.

The judge looked at Donaldson. "How do you feel about releasing Mr. Clancy on personal recognizance?"

Donaldson scowled. "Though I would prefer not to, I have not been able to identify any assets, Your Honor."

Judge Kemper studied Clancy. "You're a lucky man. If it wasn't the holiday season I'd have you be a guest of the county until you came up with some resources." He focused on Henderson. "I'm relying on you to get your client to any future hearings."

Elizabeth was pretty sure Henderson gulped as he agreed.

SHE HURRIED BACK TO THE station after the hearing. Herbie and Just Juice might seem like buffoons, but if Clancy was telling the truth, they killed Louella Belle and covered it up. Of course, they might have reported her death right way if Clancy hadn't 'helped' them.

She reminded herself that it didn't matter what the circumstances were after Clancy showed up in the laundromat. Herbie and Just Juice had not rendered aid to a badly injured woman – or called for an ambulance. No excuse for that.

Ten-thirty. She called Skelly as she walked.

"Good morning, Chief. How's my patient?"

"Frisky, except she doesn't seem to want to jump. I put a stool next to my bed so she can get up there more easily."

"Aha. Now I know who you're with at night."

Elizabeth flushed. "In the station conference room I have a couple suspects for Louella Belle's murder. Wondered if you had anything more on her."

Skelly's tone became businesslike. "Heard that. Not on the death itself, except what I told you about the amount of water in her lungs. Close to negligible. She could have been dead when she was dunked, and any water entered her lungs almost as a reflex when someone leaned her over the laundry tub."

"Poor woman."

"If I were a defense attorney, I'd try to get me to say on the stand that I think she was deceased before they pushed her head into that tub. Would make the killer look less callous."

"Less evil. I figure they'll try to say they panicked. I take it you know who I have in for questioning."

"Hammer told me."

Elizabeth swore softly.

Skelly laughed. "He'd never tell me anything he shouldn't."

Elizabeth had almost reached the station. "Any more on Stanley?"

"It'll be awhile before I get DNA information from what was under his fingernails."

"You're pretty sure it was skin?"

"Yep. You know what the odds are for a match, though…Just a sec."

Skelly apparently took the phone away from his ear and said, "I'll be right out there." To Elizabeth, he said, "I've got somebody here. Can I call you back?"

"Sure." Elizabeth hung up as she entered the station.

Hammer sat at his desk, about to bite into a donut. "How'd it go?"

"Clancy got bail. He could be back here to process out any minute." She pointed a finger at him. "Skelly says hello." She walked behind the counter into the bullpen.

Hammer flushed.

"Try to work with Clancy and his lawyer quickly and quietly. I don't want our two other guests to know he's around. Or that he's getting out."

"Roger that, Chief."

"Where's Calderone?"

"He's been talking to our guests, as you call them, to see if they qualify for a public defender. Sounds like both have mommies and daddies who could pony up, but they don't want to call them to say they're in a pickle."

Elizabeth took the last pastry from a box on Hammer's desk. "I doubt Mom and Dad would be legally required to provide money for an attorney."

"Yeah, they're both actually over twenty-one."

Calderone's voice came from around the corner, outside the conference room. "Sit tight and I'll have them send someone over." He came toward the bullpen, shaking his head as he walked in. "They're so worried about their parents finding out they need a lawyer."

"Should be worried about what they did," Hammer said.

Elizabeth pointed her donut at him. "Allegedly." She looked at Calderone. "So, it'll take a while to get a public defender attorney sent over."

"Yeah. I'll make a call from the break room so I'm not talking about it out here in front of God and everybody. Public Defender's Office doesn't usually get that much business from us." He turned toward the hallway.

"Hop to it." Elizabeth turned to Hammer. "I'm going home to change, since I'm still in yesterday's clothes and we can't talk to Jenson and Gibson for a while. Be back in an hour."

"We'll need to feed them, eventually," Hammer said.

"Sub shop delivers free." Elizabeth took a twenty from her pocket. "Get a receipt. I'll pay for theirs and get reimbursed."

She was in her car and halfway down the street before she remembered Skelly hadn't told her more about Stanley than the fingernail swabbing. She started to call him, and then figured he'd call when whoever he was dealing with left his office.

FEELING MORE HUMAN AFTER a quick shower and change of clothes, Elizabeth put out soft food for her cat. The tortoise shell had subsisted on hard food for two days and was quite peeved about it.

"I know you feel better when you try to swat me."

The cat acknowledged with one swish of her tail, without looking up from the bowl of food.

"I'll tell you what, I'll be alone in the station on Christmas. You can come to work with me."

Two tail swishes.

Elizabeth left the cat in the kitchen, and vowed to come up with a name for it by the end of the holiday week.

She kept her windshield wipers on during the ride back to the station. The precipitation was more like a heavy mist than freezing rain, but it still bunged up the wipers.

Despite the weather, cars almost clogged the streets near the town square. She guessed that people who might have finished their Christmas shopping at a mall a few miles away had decided to stay in town to shop. One good thing about the bad weather.

Elizabeth parked in front of the station and stomped on the large mat just inside the door. "Everybody awake?"

"Funny," Hammer said. "I fed the guys. Lawyers from the Office of Public Defender are with them."

She unwrapped her scarf and walked into the bullpen. "For how long?"

"Maybe half-an-hour. Came pretty quickly, especially this close to Christmas. I figured they'd have people on leave."

Calderone looked up from where he'd been typing something into his computer. "Clancy came by to pick up his watch and the few bucks he had in his pockets. I told him any funny business and we'd hand him over to the county."

"I think the judge held the bail hearing so quickly because it's just before Christmas."

Calderone grinned. "You mean maybe he's really a softie and felt sorry for Clancy?"

Elizabeth shook her head. "Hard to imagine Judge Kemper being soft on anyone. Come on back to my office. I want to figure out how we're going to handle questions with those two."

"You going to talk to them together?" Hammer asked.

Elizabeth stopped. "I think for a few minutes. That'll help us pick apart their stories when we then split them up. You think that's a good idea?"

Hammer moved his head from side to side, a seeming thinking posture. "Probably good."

"Yeah," Calderone said. "We can ask for details and compare what they say."

Elizabeth started for her office again and paused. "How many lawyers?"

Hammer smiled. "Two."

"Good. I bet they'll be sorry they have to deal with these guys."

She and Calderone entered her office and Elizabeth hung her coat on its rack. He settled across from her desk, and she sat behind it.

"Thoughts?" she asked.

"I think we can ask them to describe the afternoon in the laundry. See what they bring up about Clancy, if anything, and ask why they didn't call for an ambulance. Act as if we get what they're saying, then split them up to ask twenty more detailed questions."

Elizabeth nodded. "I like the way you think. My guess is they'll bury themselves quickly, unless their lawyers tell them to say nothing."

Down the hall, the door to the conference room opened. Elizabeth went into the hallway and raised a hand to an unknown woman who entered the hall and closed the conference room door behind her. "Do you need something like a rest room, or would you like to talk?"

"The latter, please." She approached Elizabeth and held out a hand. "Catherine Ryan, assistant public defender."

Elizabeth shook and gestured to her office. "I think you've met Officer Tony Calderone. We'll handle questioning together. Before we sit, would you like coffee?"

"I'd love a glass of water."

Hammer appeared at the doorway. "I'll grab some bottles from the fridge in the break room." He turned in that direction.

"You met Sergeant Hammer, didn't you?"

"Yes, and he pointed out what's where for us. Thanks."

Calderone stood to shake her hand, and the attorney sat next to him.

"May I call you Catherine?" Elizabeth asked.

"That's my mother's name, too, so I've always gone by Ryan."

Elizabeth sat. "Done. My guess is you want to discuss how we'll handle questioning."

A tall woman, Ryan crossed her legs and leaned back in the wood chair. "Do you plan to question them separately or together?"

"We thought we'd let them tell us the basics together and then split them, though we can separate them from the get go."

Hammer placed four water bottles on the desk. Ryan drew a breath and focused on the clock on the wall behind Elizabeth before answering. "They're pretty rattled, so together would be good."

"For a start," Calderone said.

Ryan smiled. "Get the basics and then see if they say the same things separately?"

Elizabeth did not smile. "More or less. If they're telling the truth, shouldn't be more than slight discrepancies."

Ryan nodded. "We spoke to Max Henderson. He said you're a pretty straight shooter."

Elizabeth wanted to ask her if he had relayed Clancy's narrative. "Do you have a joint defense arrangement between these two and Mr. Clancy?"

Ryan shook her head. "Not discussed. Doubt it would be. We've also suggested to Messrs. Gibson and Jenson that they use us separately."

The lack of a joint defense agreement made it less likely that Henderson had offered substantive information about what Clancy said. Elizabeth liked that and looked at Calderone. "You ready to get started?"

"Sure, Chief."

Elizabeth turned to Ryan. "Who is your colleague?"

"Norman Zakorsky. If we separate, he'll go with Mr. Jenson and I'll handle Gibson."

"Okay. Let us know what you need before we start questioning."

Neither Elizabeth or Calderone said anything until the conference room door shut behind Ryan. Calderone raised his eyebrows at Elizabeth. "Why didn't she want us to question them together the whole time?"

"Each will have his own attorney. My guess is lawyers will play our two brilliant scholars against each other."

Calderone stood. "My guess is brilliance won't come into it."

CHAPTER TWENTY-SIX

AS ELIZABETH AND CALDERONE WAITED in her office, she buzzed Hammer. "Can you bring me Louella Belle's hat? It's in the evidence locker."

He sounded surprised. "Sure."

"What do you want that for?" Calderone asked.

"I want those two to remember they killed a real person."

"So, the hat is kind of a tear jerker?"

Hammer walked in with the hat in its plastic evidence bag. "A tear-jerker hat?"

Elizabeth took it. "I'm hoping it'll make them really, really nervous."

The conference room smelled faintly of the cold-cut sandwiches Hammer had provided the two men, and more strongly of body odor. The kind Elizabeth associated with nervous sweat.

Ryan and Zakorsky sat next to their clients, with Zakorsky between Gibson and Jenson. Elizabeth wondered if the arrangement was meant to prevent the two suspects from talking directly to one another during questioning.

Elizabeth placed the hat on a small credenza behind the conference table. Ryan and Zakorsky ignored it. Gibson and Jenson seemed transfixed by its appearance.

"Before we start," Ryan said, "let's be clear that Mr. Jenson and Mr. Gibson are here voluntarily, with the intention of providing closure for this unfortunate incident."

Unfortunate incident? Elizabeth thought the euphemism was the definition of minimization.

Zakorsky added, "They believe they can speed the investigation, and I hope you'll consider their cooperation."

Elizabeth stared at Zakorsky. "As you know, I don't determine whether to press any charges, but I do let the Office of State's Attorney know who was helpful to us."

All four heads across from her nodded.

Elizabeth looked from one suspect to the other. "Gentlemen, I appreciate that you signed forms with Sergeant Hammer agreeing to tape this interview." She pressed record on the ancient taping equipment. "I thought we could begin with your description of what happened in the laundromat five nights ago."

"Don't you ask us questions?" Herbie Hiccup Gibson asked.

"Okay, please start by telling us what time you got to the laundromat and what ensued that evening."

When Just Juice 'Erasmus' Jenson looked toward Gibson, Zakorsky sat forward a little, so he blocked direct eye contact.

"Mr. Jenson?" Elizabeth asked.

"We, uh, had three baskets of dirty clothes."

"And some sheets," Herbie said.

Jenson looked at the hat, then back at Elizabeth, and nodded. "So, we put 'em all in the washers, and transferred them to a couple of dryers."

"You don't need as many dryers as washers," Herbie added.

"About what time was this?" Calderone asked.

"We got there, maybe four o'clock," Jenson said. "I didn't look at my watch, or my phone, so I can't say exactly when we walked in."

When he didn't continue, Elizabeth said, "Go on."

"So, um, Miz Simpson came in maybe half-an-hour later."

"Right after we started the dryers," Herbie said. "We had just sat down to wait for stuff to dry."

"Did she speak to you?" Calderone asked.

Jenson grunted. "She didn't…I mean, she always spoke when she saw you."

Final Cycle

"Keep going," Elizabeth said. "Tell us what you talked about, what part of the room you were in."

Herbie Gibson looked sideways, at Ryan, then back at Elizabeth. "So, she mostly talked. Whenever she saw us she said we, uh, needed to lose weight."

"She said it more insulting though," Jenson said. "Always called me Tubby, and she called Herbie Mister Fatso."

"And how did you respond?" Calderone asked.

"We usually can walk away and don't say anything. But we had our clothes there," Herbie said. "So we walked to the back, by the big laundry sink." He looked for a moment as if he would be sick, but then sat up straighter.

"Anyway," Jenson said, "she walked around the place for a couple of minutes. Looked behind the trash cans, under tables. Stuff like that."

"Did she pick up anything?" Elizabeth asked.

Both men shook their heads. "No, just looked. She's always kind of…nosy," Herbie said.

When they stopped talking, Calderone said, "Go on."

"So, she comes back to us," Jenson said. "And she starts saying what lousy parents we must have. Like they gave us too much junk food. Other insulting stuff."

"We kind of moved toward the wall, by the tub." Herbie said. "Couldn't really get too far away from her."

"And then," Jenson's voice weakened, "she came up to me and stuck her finger in my chest, and said she knew who my mother was, she'd seen her with me in the diner one time. You know, sometimes my parents came to college to visit."

Herbie said, "See, she provoked him, and…"

Ryan spoke firmly. "Mr. Gibson. Let him finish."

"She said…she said, my mother was a fat pig, just like me." Jenson looked at the table, then back at Elizabeth. When his head came up, tears had welled in his eyes. "I…I love my mother."

No one said anything. Elizabeth thought the body odor smell increased.

Jenson whispered, "I, I didn't think. I reached my hands out, and I shoved her."

After a few seconds of silence, Elizabeth said, "And then what?"

Zakorsky interrupted. "I believe my client has made it clear that he had no intention of harming Ms. Simpson."

"Actually, he hasn't," Elizabeth said. "Why don't you let him continue?"

Zakorsky reddened, and nodded at Jenson.

"I know I shouldn't have shoved her. See, my mother has diabetes. She isn't a fat pig."

Elizabeth nodded, but said nothing.

"Miz Simpson kind of leaned backwards, and then when she was straightening back up, I guess there was water on the floor. Her foot, um, I guess her right one, went up and she fell back."

"We both reached for her," Herbie said. "But we didn't catch her in time."

Jenson whispered, "It wasn't a loud sound, but it was awful. Like a crunch. And she just, she slid down the front of the laundry sink thing." He put one hand over his eyes and brushed aside a couple of tears.

Jenson drew a deep breath. "We went right over to her. I yelled, I think. Her name. I wanted her to open her eyes."

Calderone looked at Herbie Gibson. "What did you do?"

"I didn't know what to do. I started to touch her a couple of times, then I pulled my hand back. I didn't know if I should."

Elizabeth remembered Clancy saying one of the men had been flapping his hands. "Was anyone else in the laundromat at that time?"

Herbie sat up straighter. "That's right when Finn Clancy came in."

Jenson nodded. "The door opened. The alley door. Big draft."

"He said, 'Jesus, what the F did you do?' Real loud," Herbie said. "You, uh, know what the F means, right?"

Elizabeth nodded, saying nothing.

"And then?" Calderone asked.

"Clancy, he comes over, and he puts his fingers on her neck," Jenson began.

"Like on TV," Herbie said.

"And I don't think he felt a pulse, because he says, 'are you out of your effing minds? She's an old lady.' And then he was kind of quiet." Jenson drew a deep breath. "And none of us said anything for maybe twenty seconds. I don't really know how long."

Zakorsky said, "At that time, my client believed that Ms. Simpson was deceased."

Elizabeth nodded. "I suppose my biggest question is why didn't you dial 9-1-1 at that point?"

Both men nodded, and in tandem said, "We should have."

"So why not?" Calderone asked.

"I guess you could say Finn Clancy took charge," Herbie said. "Sitting here, being all logical, it seems…crazy. Why did we listen to him? I mean, I guess it was the shock of the whole thing. I, uh, does she have kids or anything? We could apologize."

Elizabeth stopped herself from asking if they thought that would really help. "And what do you mean about Mr. Clancy taking charge?"

Jenson hung his head as he spoke. "He said he could help us figure out what to do. You know, so no one would ever know we…I pushed her."

With far more emotion than Finn Clancy had shown, Just Juice Jenson and Herbie Hiccup Gibson described filling the laundry tub and lifting Louella Belle from the floor. They placed her head and shoulders in the sink.

"But, she didn't react," Herbie said.

"She was dead. I mean, really dead," Jenson said.

In a clipped tone, Calderone asked, "And then what?"

"So, we pushed her over to the dryer. The one that had dry clothes in it."

It took several minutes for Herbie and Just Juice to describe how they decided to use a laundry cart to move her. All three men loaded her in the dryer, with Clancy having the idea to put the checkered tablecloth over her face.

"And all this time, no one else came in?" Elizabeth asked.

They shook their heads, and Herbie said, "The stores around were closed. I mean, the diner was open, I guess. But you know, when it's cold, the windows over there are foggy."

Elizabeth straightened her shoulders. She'd noticed that many times. Why hadn't she thought of that earlier?

"Clancy was with you all this time?" Calderone asked.

Herbie, who had been uncharacteristically quiet for a minute, said, "Actually, that's when he left. When we got her in the dryer."

"And you?" Elizabeth asked.

Jenson said, "Our clothes were pretty much dry, so we used a couple towels to wipe the floor. And us."

No one said anything for several seconds, until Elizabeth said, "I think you might have left out one part."

Zakorsky stirred, and Elizabeth held up one hand, palm in his direction. "Did Finn Clancy help you from the goodness of his heart?"

Herbie snorted. "Not hardly. He wanted five hundred dollars. We said we'd pay it."

Jenson nodded. "We went to the bank the next morning and used our debit and credit cards to get it."

Five hundred dollars. The price of covering up a senseless killing.

CHAPTER TWENTY-SEVEN

ELIZABETH AND CALDERONE LEFT the seemingly sorrowful killers with their lawyers about two PM and returned to her office. She shut the door. "If they had called 9-1-1 the heaviest charge could have been involuntary manslaughter."

Calderone shrugged. "Better for them, but Louella Belle would still be dead."

"Of course." She picked up her phone and buzzed Hammer. "They told us pretty much the same story as Clancy, in terms of hiding her body."

"So how did her neck get broken?" Hammer asked.

"Jenson pushed her after Louella Belle called his mother a fat pig. They're going to talk to their lawyers for a few minutes, then we'll split them up."

"Gotcha," Hammer said. "Can I tell the others?"

"For now, just say that their version coincided with Clancy's. I don't want a lot of discussion."

"Speaking of discussion, Jerry Pew called. He knows Clancy's out, and wants to know why two public defenders are over here on a Saturday."

Calderone had been able to hear Hammer. "Radio station'll be next."

Elizabeth frowned. "Are there no secrets in this town?"

"That's whaddya call it, rhetorical, right?" Hammer asked.

She raised and lowered both eyebrows twice. "Yes. When he calls back, tell him I will talk to him, but not until later this afternoon. If he gives you a hard time, remind him I know he's not on deadline." She hung up.

Calderone stood. "We have the tapes, but I took some notes. I'll start writing them up and you can look at them."

Before he reached the door, someone knocked quietly. "Chief Friedman?"

"It's open, Ms. Ryan. Come in."

Calderone took his seat again.

Elizabeth gestured to a chair next to Calderone.

"I know we agreed you'd interview them separately next, but we've just learned something else you may want to know."

Elizabeth raised her eyebrows.

"Not specifically related to Ms. Simpson, some things that go on, or went on, in the laundromat."

Elizabeth stood. "Sure." She glanced at Calderone. "Join me, please."

When they were all seated in their respective places in the conference room, Elizabeth said, "What's up, gentlemen?"

Herbie began. "So, do you maybe know why Finn Clancy came in the laundromat's back door?"

"I will if you tell me," Elizabeth said.

"So, sometimes he sold stuff there," Jenson said. "Didn't want people to pay a lot of attention to him."

"What kind of stuff?" Calderone asked.

Herbie said, "As far as I know, it's all pot, in little baggies."

"I mean," Just Juice said, "you can buy it legal now, but it's still cheaper to get it home-grown."

"And better," Herbie said.

"May we strike that last point?" Ryan asked.

Elizabeth smiled. "It's not a trial, Ryan, but I won't infer anything from what Mr. Gibson said."

Zakorsky frowned. "I advised Mr. Jenson that this information is not pertinent to this case, but they insisted on talking to you about it."

"We want to help," Herbie said, and Just Juice nodded both of his chins.

"After Ms. Simpson's death, I learned that a couple of people had found empty baggies on the premises, though not often," Elizabeth said.

"Clancy grow it?" Calderone asked.

Both men shrugged. Herbie said, "Sometimes he sleeps in the woods."

Though Clancy could have been guarding plants, hikers traipsed through the local woods a lot. Somehow Elizabeth didn't think home-grown meant the edge of Logland.

"Just Clancy sell the stuff?" Elizabeth asked.

Jenson shook his head. "That guy Wessley kind of worked with Clancy on it. I think he provided the baggies. Not sure about if he grew the stuff."

So much for Blake Wessley being a reformed rabble-rouser.

Elizabeth studied her notepad and then looked from Herbie to Just Juice. "I just have one more question. Which one of you has the baseball pitcher's arm?"

"Excuse me?" Ryan asked.

"What are you talking about?" Zakorsky asked.

Herbie and Just Juice studied the table top.

Before Elizabeth could ask another question, Hammer opened the conference room door, without knocking. "Chief, you're needed at the hospital."

She half-turned to look at Hammer. "Can't you handle it?"

"Uh, one of the docs is hurt. They want you."

ELIZABETH KEPT HERSELF FROM stomping on the accelerator, and pulled into the spot near the hospital ER that was reserved for law enforcement. She ran inside. Before she got to the receptionist, the woman pointed toward the locked doors to the treatment area and activated a buzzer to let her in.

She walked more slowly as she approached the ER nurses' station, and locked eyes with the older nurse who was often on duty in the evening. Her badge reminded Elizabeth that her name was Frances.

"Evening, Chief. Doctor is with Skelly, but he'll be out in a minute, and you can go in." The nurse nodded to her left.

"What happened to him? Sergeant Hammer said he was injured somehow."

"I'm not sure. He had a head injury, and I believe it was not from a fall. He's kind of in and out of consciousness, but some of that might be the medicine." The phone near the nurse buzzed, and she picked it up and started talking.

Elizabeth sat on a stool on wheels and nudged it back to the wall so she could lean against it. Her heart beat less wildly now than it had a few minutes ago, and she drew a deep breath. *You need to put your cop hat on. What the hell happened to Skelly?*

A man's voice called, "Chief Friedman?"

Elizabeth recognized him as Dr. Evan Jessup, the hospital's medical director. Not someone she usually ran into in the emergency room. She stood and walked toward him. "Yes. How is he?"

Jessup did not smile. "Better than he was. He took a hard blow, but no skull fracture."

Her heart rate went up again. "I'd like to see him, and then I'll get someone else down here."

In a weaker-than-usual voice, Skelly called from his curtained cubicle. "Mahan's been in."

For a second anger rose, but she tamped it down. Mahan had waited to call Hammer until he knew what was going on.

Jessup pulled aside the curtain and indicated that Elizabeth should enter the cubicle. When she did, he pulled it shut and did not follow her.

Hands on her hips, Elizabeth surveyed Skelly. "This is quite a pickle you've gotten into, Ollie."

He smiled weakly at the Laurel and Hardy joke. "You're dating yourself."

"Are you kidding? That's classic comedy." She stood next to the gurney and grew somber. "What happened?"

He shut his eyes, but spoke. "I got off the phone with you because someone came into my suite, as you call it. I walked out of my office, and the guy was pulling a ski mask over his face."

"There to steal drugs?" she asked.

"There because he wanted the skin samples from Stanley Buttons. Very angry when I said they'd been sent elsewhere for examination."

"Good God." Elizabeth sat in a small plastic chair next to the gurney. "And he hit you? With what? Are you okay?"

"Big lump, mild concussion as you measure those. Blinding headache. Oh, double vision, so if I'm not looking you in the eye, you'll know why."

"A man? For sure?"

"Yeah, I gave Mahan as much of a description as I could. Not much, because of the mask."

The curtain surrounding Skelly peeled back with a metal-on-metal sound. Skelly winced. Elizabeth turned around.

Mahan looked sheepish. "Chief, I thought I should wait at least a few minutes, until I knew what was going on."

"Good choice." She didn't think so, but it's what she would usually do, too, unless there was immediate danger.

Elizabeth lowered her voice and spoke to Skelly. "I know you have that headache. I'll step away to talk to Mahan, and then come back."

She left the cubicle and walked a few yards away. She and Mahan stood next to a wall. "Did Skelly tell you what the perp used to hit him?"

"All he saw was a piece of wood, but like a handle. He thought the end the attacker held in his hand was some kind of tool. The guy held the tool end and walloped Skelly with the handle."

Elizabeth filed that away. Maybe she'd suggest Skelly take a walk through the hardware store when he felt better.

"What kind of description did you get?"

Mahan glanced at his pocket-sized notebook. "Sketchy. Sounds like a slim guy, maybe just under six feet. Skelly bases that on the fact that he was about as tall as the guy's chin." He looked up from his notes. "So if Skelly's roughly five-nine, maybe the guy's about six-two?"

"Could be. Clothes? The guy's coloring?"

"Clothes were dark, hands were gloved, and the ski mask, of course."

He started to say more, but Elizabeth raised a finger. Something flitted in and out of her brain. She snapped her fingers. "Slight build, maybe same height. Sounds like a man who was in Hy-Vee when Stanley Buttons was. But he wasn't wearing a ski mask."

"Who saw him?" Mahan asked.

"A young clerk named Kimberly. At this point, I'd like her to come to the station to look at our book of local mug shots. Before this, nothing about the guy seemed that unusual. He's a customer she's seen there before."

"So, we should ask her to come down?"

"She's maybe eighteen, could be seventeen. I'd like her parents with her. Calderone's met her." Elizabeth shut her eyes for a second. "We have Herbie and Just Juice and their attorneys in the conference room. We won't call her to come down until we're done with them. Let Hammer know I'll be back in a few minutes."

Elizabeth walked back into Skelly's cubicle. "I feel bad, but I've got two murderers in the conference room, so I have to get back. What can I get you?"

"I'd say heavy painkillers, but I'm sure someone else will provide them. Can you turn off the overhead light?"

"Sure." Elizabeth did that. A small fluorescent bulb above a sink provided enough light. She stood next to Skelly's gurney. "They won't let you go home tonight, will they?"

"Nope."

"Have any fish that need to be fed?" she asked.

Skelly smiled, but without opening his eyes. "No to that, too."

"If they let you out tomorrow, I'll take you home. Or…you can sleep on my couch. I do owe you Christmas Eve dinner."

"Damn. I'll make sure they let me out tomorrow."

WHEN SHE ARRIVED AT the station, Hammer motioned that she should come to his desk. If she hadn't been upset about Skelly, she would have laughed at his furtive gesture. "What's up?"

"The woman attorney, Ryan I think it is," Hammer said.

"Yes."

"She said they're working on confessions. Want to work out some sort of deal."

"That's not up to me."

Hammer nodded. "They called someone at the local office of the State's Attorney."

"Damn it, we haven't gotten to Stanley Buttons yet."

"She started to say something about that, but then she said to call her when you got back."

Elizabeth nodded. "How ticked were they when I left?"

He shrugged. "I told 'em it was the medical examiner got hurt. The guy, Zakorsky, said something about what's Logland coming to?"

"I wish I knew." Elizabeth walked to the conference room and knocked lightly. When she walked in, the smell of nervous men almost overwhelmed her. She left the door to the hallway open.

"I'm truly sorry to have left."

"How's Skelly?" Calderone asked.

"Concussion." She took in the two attorneys. "I hear you want to talk to the State's Attorney staff?"

Ryan nodded. "If you will assign someone to accompany Mr. Gibson and Mr. Jenson, I think it would make more sense to meet over there." She hesitated. "Forms and such to sign are in the computers there."

"Sure. We're going to be stretched thin here for a few hours. I'm going to ask if their security staff can take over while your clients are in that office."

Elizabeth glanced at Herbie and Just Juice. She had seen them in the Bully Pulpit as jovial college guys. They would never be that again.

Herbie cleared his throat. "Chief, uh, I'm sorry about your window. You want me to fix it?"

Elizabeth ignored him and turned her attention to Calderone. "Unless we get another emergency in the next few minutes, I'd like you to accompany Mr. Jenson and Mr. Gibson, and then come back. I'll hang out in here for a few minutes so you can gather what you need."

A tired-looking Calderone stood from his seat at the table. "Good idea."

As he left, Elizabeth turned to Zakorsky. "You've already talked to someone in Donaldson's office?"

Both attorneys said yes.

Elizabeth turned to Herbie and Just Juice. "You don't need me to tell you how much easier this would have been if you'd have called us when it happened."

Herbie nodded. "We panicked."

Ryan added, "And got bad advice."

"They should be able to tell the difference between good and bad advice." Elizabeth again looked from Ryan to Zakorsky. "I'm figuring that last bit of discussion we had before I left may seem like a bargaining chip to you. I'm not waiting to act on it, but I'll acknowledge where I got the information when the time comes."

Hammer came in with four bottles of water. "Calderone will be about five minutes, maybe ten." He placed the bottles on the table.

"I need to step out to work on the hospital injury. If you need me before you leave, just let Sergeant Hammer know."

"Thank you, Chief," Ryan said.

Elizabeth thought a thank-you from Herbie and Just Juice was in order, but it wasn't forthcoming. She shut the door to the conference room and walked toward her office. Hammer stood outside it.

"Where's Calderone?" she asked.

"Gargling. He said the room stunk, and he thought the swishing might help get the smell outta his sinuses."

Elizabeth grinned. "It is rank in there."

Calderone walked out of the staff restroom, next to the break room. "I've questioned all kinds of perps, but those guys smell worse than all the others put together."

"Sorry I had to leave."

"Skelly okay?"

"Concussion, massive headache, double vision. But could have been worse."

Calderone swore. "What the hell did someone want from him?"

"The skin swabs from under Buttons' fingernails."

Neither Hammer or Calderone said anything for several seconds. Then Hammer said, "I guess we know Buttons' killer is still in town."

Elizabeth nodded toward the conference room. "And the guy is thin, so it's not either of those two bozos."

CHAPTER TWENTY-EIGHT

ELIZABETH SAT AT HER DESK Saturday evening for several minutes, simply thinking. Clancy sold pot, and may have done so in conjunction with Blake Wessley. Blake Wessley was the same build as the man in Hy-Vee and the person who attacked Skelly.

Wessley had been arrested in Logland previously, so his photo was on file. She'd have Hammer pull together a page of photos of white men with brown hair and ask Kimberly to look at it. If Wessley had been in Hy-Vee the night Stanley was murdered, Kimberly would likely recognize him.

Skelly might be able to identify the shape of the man who injured him, maybe the voice. But what was he hit with?

The hospital had many security cameras. Unless the attacker had walked into the lobby with a ski mask, he took it off somewhere in the building. She dialed the hospital and asked for security.

When she identified herself and asked about cameras, the man on the phone said, "Two steps ahead of you, Chief. This is Randall Watson. We've met briefly a couple of times."

"Sure, hospital open house last year."

"Yep. I'm pulling a lot of video. We don't have much of a description, but I'm tagging everyone in dark clothes, kind of tall."

"Slim, too, I think Skelly said."

"Roger that. I'll send over a DVD in an hour or two."

"There is a chance that the same person killed Stanley Buttons. And a slight chance that I may get an ID on someone who was in the grocery store with Stanley not long before he was killed."

Watson whistled softly. "Be good if we could get it all to come together."

"And without anyone else getting hurt or killed."

ELIZABETH SAT AT HER desk at six-thirty eating a piece of cold pizza and going over notes from the day – hers and those of the other officers. Mahan had talked to hospital staff who worked in a lab of some sort that was on the basement level with the autopsy space. None had heard anything or seen anyone leaving Skelly's area at about the time he was attacked. No cameras in the basement.

She tossed the crust of her piece of cold pizza into the trash can next to her desk and stood to stretch. She'd sent Hammer and the rest of the day staff home. She would have left by now, but Kimberly Hamilton and her parents were due at seven.

Elizabeth moved to the bullpen just as someone came in the front door. Though she'd only met him once, she thought he was Randall Wilson from the hospital.

He held up an envelope about half the size of a piece of copy paper. "Thought I'd drop off the disk myself. Too big a file to email."

"That's great. Come on back." She strode to the counter and motioned to the short, swinging door that led behind the counter.

"I'm on my way home." He handed the disk across the counter to her. "I don't think you'll find much."

"No one looks like our guy?"

"One person might be. He's seen getting off the first-floor elevator at the right time, and he has on black pants and a dark parka. No ski mask, of course, but he looks down, wears a ball cap with a brim, and sunglasses."

Elizabeth accepted the disk. "Sunglasses?"

"Didn't look that odd, since he was headed toward the exit. Someone passing him would think he'd put them on just before leaving the building."

Elizabeth tried to tamp down her disappointment. "Get a sense of age?"

Watson shrugged. "He walks briskly, so I thought younger rather than say seventy. His face isn't visible at all."

Elizabeth shook her head. "Oh well...hey, I realize there is one important thing I don't know. Who found Skelly?"

Watson grinned. "He found himself. There's an internal phone on a small table next to the chairs in that small waiting room of his. I heard he never really lost consciousness. Pulled the phone to the floor by its cord and dialed the hospital operator."

"That was lucky."

Watson nodded. "At least he didn't have a long trip to the ER."

KIMBERLY HAMILTON AND BOTH parents arrived at the station about seven o'clock.

"I really appreciate you folks coming in on a Saturday evening," Elizabeth said.

"Anything to keep this moving," Kimberly's father said.

On the conference room table, Elizabeth had placed a thermal pitcher of hot water, tea bags, sugar, and hot chocolate. She wanted to put the young woman and her parents at ease.

Kimberly glanced at the table. "You remembered I like hot chocolate."

Elizabeth smiled. In fact, she had forgotten that's what they had drunk at Hy-Vee. "We appreciate your help, it's the least I can do."

Kimberly's father had a florid face and thinning hair. His rumpled clothes said fifty, but his relatively unlined face put him closer to forty. "We don't mind helping, but our biggest concern is whether Kimberly is in any danger."

"I don't believe so. Even if the man she saw in the store is the person who attacked Stanley Buttons, he won't associate Kimberly with any actions we take."

"But she may have to testify," Kimberly's mother said. Worry lines etched deep in her forehead indicated the woman focused on many concerns.

"A slight chance. I may be off base, but there is someone I've recently connected to some other activities in town. If it's the same person, I can bring him in without ever mentioning Kimberly."

Mr. Hamilton sat back in his chair, and Mrs. Hamilton released a sigh.

Elizabeth turned to Kimberly. "You ready to look at a page of photographs?"

She nodded, with enthusiasm. "I want to help."

From a file folder in front of her, Elizabeth took a legal-sized piece of paper. On it were a number of photos. Two besides Blake Wessley were local, but most were mug shots Hammer had pulled from elsewhere. One was a Hollywood stunt man. Elizabeth had no idea where Hammer got that photo.

"Now, I want you to take your time." She placed the page in front of Kimberly. "You don't need to rush…"

"That's him. Top row, in the middle. That's the man who was in Hy-Vee that night."

Blake Wessley's unsmiling photo sat squarely under Kimberly Hamilton's index finger, and she wore a big smile.

WHEN SHE CALLED TO EXPLAIN the situation, the perpetually nervous Dollar General manager had more questions.

"Sir, all you have to do is give Blake Wessley a chore that will take him to the back of the store. You will have already let Grayson and Mahan in through the back entrance, and they'll be in the storage room."

"And where will I be?" Howard asked.

"Since you said it's just you two in the store now and it's almost closing, when Wessley gets to the back of the store, they'll confront him and tell him his only option is to accompany them to the police station. If you want, you can leave the store, but I suggest you simply wait in your office if you don't want to stay on the selling floor."

"It'll be terrible publicity!"

Final Cycle

Elizabeth tried to make her tight smile a reassuring one. "We'll try not to handcuff him in the store, but if he gives any indication of resistance, we'll have to."

After a few more of his questions, Elizabeth wanted to suggest that Howard wear what TV ads called discreet protection, available in the diaper aisle.

Elizabeth stayed in the station when Grayson and Mahan went to Dollar General. She had briefed the mayor and asked her to sit on the information until tomorrow, in case Wessley wasn't their man. But she knew he was.

The station seemed almost eerily quiet after the activity of having Clancy in a cell, questioning Herbie and Just Juice, and working with Kimberly and her parents.

She still found it hard to believe that Blake Wessley had killed Stanley and attacked Skelly. She had thought him conceited and irresponsible, then seen him as trying to change. She would never have pegged him for such violent crimes.

The station phone rang and she answered it.

"Chief, Jerry Pew here."

"Ah, Jerry. Looking for more ways to say we aren't doing squat?"

"Now, Chief, there wasn't anything to tell. I hear now there is now."

"Did Avery Maxwell get hold of you?"

Pew's tone grew formal. "If you don't mind, Chief, I'd rather not say."

Elizabeth smiled to herself. She bet Jerry Pew had at least one new orifice. "We'll put out a formal press release, maybe even tomorrow. I know you aren't on deadline."

He almost whined. "Chief, that's Christmas Eve! Can't you give me anything?"

"I need your agreement not to post anything on your web page tonight."

Silence.

"Jerry, I'm serious. I need to work out several details. If you can't guarantee that you won't print on paper or the web until tomorrow, then we're done talking."

"Okay, okay!"

"Two college students have confessed to the unintended killing of Louella Belle Simpson, and a very stupid effort to hide her body in a dryer. When we issue the release, you'll know their names, and after you read the release you can call me with questions."

"What about Finn Clancy? You had him in there."

"At this point, I believe we'll refer to him as an accessory after the fact. And you damn well better not use that now, either."

His tone grew haughty. "The people have a right to know."

"Most of the people in Logland are getting ready for bed. Tomorrow is plenty of time. If you don't sit on this, it'll be a lot harder for you to keep the people in the know in the future."

"All right, all right." Pew hung up.

Elizabeth cleaned empty food wrappers and scraps of paper from the conference room table and thought about calling the hospital to check on Skelly. She decided he would be sleeping, and she didn't really have time for a conversation on any topic other than solving Stanley Buttons' murder. And the attack on Skelly, of course.

The phone rang again, and Matt Howard told her Mahan and Grayson were on the way to the station with Blake Wessley. "I still can't believe it, Chief. I worked with him, just the two of us, several days a week. I could be dead."

Elizabeth rolled her eyes. "Good that you're still with us, Mr. Howard. Thanks for the call."

Mahan's cruiser pulled up in front of the station, and he and Grayson got out. Mahan then opened the back door and a handcuffed Blake Wessley emerged. He must have given them a hard time.

Elizabeth opened the station door without saying anything, and locked it when the men were inside. "Conference room, gentlemen."

"Chief Friedman," Wessley began, "this is ridic…"

"Put a cork in it, Mr. Wessley."

After ten minutes of questioning, Elizabeth knew Blake Wessley would tell them nothing quickly. She stared directly into his eyes. "I don't understand your reluctance to provide any information. I'm simply asking about any contact you may have had with Stanley Buttons the night he died."

Final Cycle

Wessley's jaw clenched and unclenched. "And I've told you I don't know the man."

No law said Elizabeth had to be fully truthful in questioning a suspect. "Come on, you guys came within a few inches of each other in the grocery store the night Mr. Buttons died."

"I was preoccupied. I didn't notice anyone."

"The store has cameras," Calderone said.

Elizabeth was pleased he had picked up on her ploy.

Wessley looked from one to the other. "He was a nosy old man who tried to mind other people's business. But he was nobody to me."

"Maybe he noticed you and Finn Clancy selling pot in the laundromat," Elizabeth said.

Wessley said nothing.

"We aren't running a boarding house here, so Officers Mahan and Grayson will drop you at the county jail for the night. We can resume tomorrow."

He shouted. "I'm not going to jail! I want a lawyer!"

Elizabeth kept her tone neutral. "As we told you, you can have one. I can hold you for selling pot without a distributor's license, and we'll sort out the really nasty stuff tomorrow. It's been a long day."

When Mahan, Grayson, and Blake Wessley left, Elizabeth stared at her phone for several minutes. She wanted a call from the woman at All Eyes on You. If it didn't show Buttons and Wessley interacting, it could show a malevolent stare from Wessley. *I must be really tired.*

Her cell phone rang, and she recognized Hammer's home number. "Everything okay, sergeant?"

"Better than. I gave the woman from All Eyes on You my cell phone number, and she just called."

"Late. Thanks for being so diligent."

"You can thank her later. When Buttons was in the back of the store, near the dairy stuff I think she said, the man she describes as wearing pressed jeans turned from an aisle and they looked at each other."

"Any conversation?"

"Didn't seem to be, and she'll send over the DVD. What she did notice was that Stanley seemed nervous to see Wessley. He had just taken a pound of butter from the refrigerator case and he dropped it. Then he hurried to the check-out."

Elizabeth pictured Stanley Buttons the day she had talked to him and Grace. At one point he closed his eyes, and she wondered if he'd been trying to remember something. Maybe he had seen Finn Clancy and Blake Wessley exchanging money or plastic baggies, but didn't want to get involved."

"Chief?" Hammer asked.

"I'm here. Good to show them near each other, and that Stanley seemed nervous. I suppose it's too much to have expected an argument where we could read their lips."

"Okay, I thanked her pretty good."

"Great. When we get the video we can check to be sure it's Blake Wessley who worried Stanley, but it sure sounds like it."

CHAPTER TWENTY-NINE

THE MORNING OF CHRISTMAS EVE, Elizabeth stopped by County State's Attorney Donaldson's office in the courthouse. Sunday was a rare day for him to be there. In an odd way, the cheery decorations in his outer office reminded her that Stanley's son would not have another Christmas with his father.

Donaldson was in no rush to get a confession from Blake Wessley. "It's not just Sunday, it's Christmas Eve, Chief. And the guy is off the streets. I've gone over what you summarized for me, and talked to Judge Kemper. Wessley's parents are going to provide an attorney, and I said the guy can meet with Wessley anytime."

"Will you get beyond the period where you can hold him without charging him with anything?"

"Could be, but when they booked him, the corrections staff saw scratches on his right wrist, which they photographed. He had on a shirt with longer sleeves to cover them. Between that and the girl's ID, it could be the basis for you to arrest him on a new charge. We can hold him for a bail hearing on the twenty-sixth."

"I'd like to get a search warrant for his apartment."

"Today? On Christmas Eve?" Donaldson asked.

"Yes, he could tell his parents to go in there and remove something."

"What do you expect to find?

"Maybe the knife that killed Stanley Buttons. Maybe the piece of wood used to hit Skelly." She described what Skelly said. "I've been thinking it could be one of those hand-held weeders. They sell them at Dollar General."

"In the winter?"

Elizabeth shrugged. "We need to get in there before someone else does."

"Okay. You get it typed up and I assume Judge Kemper will allow the warrant."

Elizabeth stopped in the courthouse lobby to call Calderone about working up a request for a warrant. "Talk to Mahan, in case I missed something about how Skelly described what he thinks hit him." She paused. "In the Buttons autopsy report, Skelly gave an opinion about the type of knife used to kill the poor man."

Calderone added, "I suppose you could add paraphernalia to package and sell pot, since Jenson and Gibson said Wessley was somehow in on that with Clancy."

"Not sure the word of two suspected killers will be enough to add the pot stuff to the search," Elizabeth said.

"That's okay," Calderone said. "It'll give Judge Kemper a chance to throw out part of the warrant. He likes to do that."

"Cynic. I'll be at the station in about forty-five minutes."

"Before you hang up, Chief." Calderone paused for several seconds. "Writing the warrant request is straightforward, but the one thing that's absent is clear motive. Why would Wessley kill Stanley just because he saw the guy sell pot? Thirty years ago, maybe. Not now."

"It does seem strange, and more so that he'd have a weapon handy. But he's self-centered and used to getting his own way. He's also on thin ice with his parents, and on probation. A pot conviction might put him in jail and cause him to lose any monetary support from his parents."

"I suppose. I'll have a draft warrant when you're back here." Calderone hung up.

She left the courthouse and drove to the senior apartment building. If Grace was not in the lobby, she would call her. She also needed to call Stanley's son to tell him they were making progress. She decided she'd let Skelly talk to Steve Buttons about the apparent cancer his father had. A minister might call that a comfort, and maybe it would be. Not to Elizabeth.

She thought of closure as the best kind of comfort. Progress might seem like small consolation, but it could make Christmas slightly less dismal for the two people most upset about Stanley's death.

If only someone cared as much about Louella Belle Simpson.

BACK AT THE STATION, Hammer handed her a note to call Louella Belle's attorney, John Stone. And two messages from Jerry Pew.

"What did Stone want?"

Hammer shrugged. "You know him. He never says."

Elizabeth dialed Stone. As he answered, she could envision him sitting in his older wooden office chair. It always squeaked as he sat back in it.

"Morning, Chief," Stone said. "I filed Louella Belle's will at the courthouse Friday, but I headed out of the office before I thought to call you. I have a copy for you that I'll send over."

"That's great. I'll stop by, or one of the officers will. Anything especially important?"

"Nothing that relates to her death. She left all of her assets to two places."

"And they were?"

"There's a little-known poison control function in the county Office of Public Health. She left a decent amount to develop literature and do classroom visits about food safety."

When Elizabeth said nothing, Stone continued. "The bulk goes to the summer lunch program, which is a United Way effort. Guess they wish they could do more. Louella Belle hoped the interest would be enough to fund lunch every day, all summer. With mostly organic food, of course."

Elizabeth felt her eyes start to tear. "Did she tell you why such issues were important to her?"

"No, but when you called to say it would be good to remove that scrapbook and the items on the shelf with it, I went to her house."

"So sad," Elizabeth said.

"Yes." Stone hesitated.

Elizabeth sensed he had more to say. "What else sir?"

"She was worth a lot of money."

"How much?"

"One million, two hundred thousand dollars, give or take."

Elizabeth sat up straighter. "How does a retired teacher amass that much money?"

"My guess is she never felt she had anyone to spend it on," Stone said.

WHEN THE WARRANT CAME through early Sunday afternoon, Elizabeth went to Wessley's apartment with Calderone and Mahan. She didn't want anything missed, as Louella Belle's hat had been at the laundromat.

She had made a list of objects that she wanted them to look for – potential weapons, of course, a dark ball cap, indications of pot supplies, and a ski mask. When she passed them to Calderone and Mahan, she said, "Be creative. Maybe something else will jump out at you."

Elizabeth had been in the now-closed fraternity when Wessley lived there, but had no reason to have visited his one-bedroom apartment on the top floor of a dress shop on the town square. The apartment was locked, and Wessley had not been willing to provide a key.

Before she had officers damage a door frame, Elizabeth asked the dress shop owner downstairs if she knew the landlord. She did.

The sixty-plus landlord was found at the grocery store, buying cans of pumpkin for his wife. "Thanks for calling to get a key, Chief. Saves me repairing the door. Never had anything like this from a tenant before." He took a quick look at the search warrant and let them in.

"We'll call you when we leave so you can lock up," Elizabeth said.

"Turn the lock on the handle, then I don't have to run right back to do the deadbolt." As he walked down the stairs, he muttered, "Can't trust anybody these days."

Mahan shrugged at Elizabeth and he and Calderone followed her into the unit. Rarely did the phrase 'neat as a pin' apply to the apartments of men she knew, but they fit Blake Wessley's place. Even the placemats on a small dining room table were precisely aligned.

The three did a brief walk-through first. One bedroom with a walk-in closet, small kitchen, large bathroom, and a living-dining room combo.

"Each one of us will do each space separately," Elizabeth said. "If you need help moving furniture or whatever, ask. Then leave it pushed aside for the next person."

Mahan flexed his arm muscles and Elizabeth rolled her eyes.

They worked in silence until Calderone called from the bathroom. "Got it."

Elizabeth and Mahan joined Calderone, who had squatted on the floor to look under the toilet tank. He looked up. "He taped the knife to the back of the tank."

"Has every man in this country seen *The Godfather*?" Elizabeth asked.

"At least twice," Mahan said.

Calderone stayed on his haunches and reached his gloved hand behind the toilet tank. He gently loosened duct tape. After twenty seconds or so, he slid the knife down the back of the toilet with one hand, and caught it with the other.

They studied it in silence until Mahan said, "I think I've seen that kind of steak knife on a display in the grocery store. You get one when you spend something like $500 in one month."

"And what?" Elizabeth asked. "He put it under his coat and went after Stanley?"

Mahan frowned. "I bet he tries to say he took it at the store that night, and it was spur-of-the moment, not planned."

Elizabeth continued to stare at the serrated blade. "Easy to hide in his coat as he left the store. But why on earth would he keep it?"

Calderone stood slowly. "I'm too old to squat like that. I can see him bringing it back here initially. He couldn't toss it near the senior apartments, and if he put it in the dumpster behind this place and it was found, it would be too close to where he lived."

"I bet he meant to take it out of town, like if he went home for Christmas," Mahan said. "Could have tossed it in one of the lakes around here."

Elizabeth shook her head. "And lucky for us, he ran out of time."

WHEN THEY WRAPPED UP at Wessley's place, Elizabeth kept turning over issues related to Finn Clancy. Yes, his interview had implicated Just Juice and Herbie Hiccup; it could have taken her a long time to get to them. The two men were such bumblers, she thought their roles would have become apparent eventually.

But did Clancy's assistance mean he should pay substantially less of a penalty than the two men who killed her? His crimes – even forgetting the probable pot sales – were less egregious, but still very serious.

She sighed to herself. Fortunately, the state's attorney made those decisions. She would continue to give Clancy credit for his help, but she would not argue hard in his behalf. That's why Clancy had an attorney.

ELIZABETH WAS READY FOR her last report to be written so she could get out of the station, but she had one more responsibility. If she hadn't invited Wally Kermit, she'd have asked her own officers if they wanted to skip Christmas cookies and eggnog in exchange for better food New Year's Eve.

She walked into Doris Minx's cookie shop at three-fifteen. "Merry Christmas, Doris. I was afraid you'd be closed on Sunday."

"Only because I had a couple late orders to finish. The last customer just left." Her baker's hat, which bore a holly leaf, jiggled in apparent excitement. "Merry Christmas to you, too, Chief. I hear we can feel safer now."

"I think so. It's been a long week, hasn't it?."

She grew somber. "I didn't much like Louella Belle, but I feel bad how she died. Very undignified." Her frown deepened. "The paper didn't say. Did she, did it hurt much?"

"From what Skelly has said, I think she had a moment of surprise, and then she wouldn't have known much, if anything."

Doris nodded slowly. "The mayor ordered a big batch of cookies to be delivered to the senior apartments this morning. It's hard to know what to do, but a bunch of those folks come by here. They like their sweets."

"That sounds lovely. Listen, Doris, I usually bake some cookies to have at the office Christmas Eve, but I've been busy."

Doris' eyebrows went up and her eyes brightened. "Oh, Elizabeth, I'd love to give you some."

"No, no. I want to buy them."

After a full minute of haggling, Elizabeth agreed to a discount on the cookies and Doris insisted on providing a large loaf of pumpkin bread as a gift.

"Thanks, Doris. We'll really enjoy all this."

She winked. "Make sure you eat the pumpkin bread today. It's day old."

As Elizabeth left the store, snow began to fall softly. On the short drive to the station, she hummed "It's Beginning to Look a Lot Like Christmas."

When she got to the station, several cars were parked in front, so she stowed the Crown Vic a couple of doors down. She hoped the people were at another business and not there to report crimes.

Laughter greeted her as she opened the door. All of her officers stood in the bullpen and the counter had a festive red tablecloth. Even better, a plate of sliced ham and cheese, rolls, and a bowl of what looked to be green bean casserole sat atop the tablecloth.

Nick grinned at her and Marti waved from near Hammer's desk, where she served eggnog to Wally as Mahan waited for his. She called, "Hey, Chief. You got them! Merry Christmas."

"This is wonderful!"

"We finished that big lunch at the diner. You know the Christmas Eve thing, and we had a lot left," Nick said.

Elizabeth placed the baked goods on the counter. "I hope you'll stay and eat with us."

"Goin' to my parents'," Nick said.

The door opened again and Alice, Gene, and Squeaky came in, brushing snow from their shoulders.

"Afternoon, everybody," Squeaky called.

"Anyone need inked for Christmas?" Gene asked, grinning.

No one answered, but from the corner of her eye, Elizabeth saw Calderone gesture toward his back side.

Alice kissed Elizabeth on the cheek. "It's going around town that you all solved the murders. We came by to say thank you."

"We should call Doris," Elizabeth said.

"I did," Hammer said, as the door opened again.

"Nobody called me," Jerry Pew said.

"You're supposed to have a nose for news," Alice said.

Elizabeth wanted to be done and go to the hospital to see if Skelly could leave, but she mingled for more than an hour. She noticed Calderone motion to Wally that his fly was down, and wondered if the man was so unmindful every day.

Hammer picked up used paper plates and cups until Mahan told him if he kept doing it he'd send all of them to Hammer's house wrapped like a Christmas present.

"I think he'd like that," Officer Taylor said. He spoke with the authority of an unlikely Santa -- tall and with hair as red as the costume he wore.

Elizabeth smiled at Hammer from across the room. "Remember, Hammer's the one who certifies your time cards to me."

CHAPTER THIRTY

AN HOUR LATER, Elizabeth parked her small Ford in the circular drive in front of the main hospital entrance and left the flashers on. She rationalized that she wasn't in front of the door and would be there only a few minutes.

The hospital lobby was deserted at five PM Christmas Eve. Hospitals limited new voluntary admissions leading up to major holidays, but she hadn't expected the place to be so quiet. She picked up the information phone on the desk and asked for the nurses' station on Skelly's floor.

"This is Elizabeth Friedman. Is Mr. Hutton ready to leave?"

The nurse laughed. "I never heard anyone call Skelly Mr. Hutton."

"Good point. Would you like me to come up, or is he being wheeled down? I may be early."

"He's ready. I'll bring him down myself." The nurse lowered her voice. "He's been chomping at the bit to leave, but if it were me, I would've wanted to stay at least one more day."

Elizabeth wasn't sure what to say. "Double vision cleared up?"

"Mostly, and he's not too dizzy. But," she paused, "I don't mean to be nosy, but do you know if anyone will be with him the next couple days?"

Elizabeth hesitated. "I told him he could share a couch with my cat."

The nurse laughed again. "That's perfect. We'll be down in five minutes."

SINCE MOVING TO LOGLAND, Elizabeth had largely kept to herself. A small-town police chief could easily know everyone her officers arrested, so she wanted some distance between her and most residents.

Skelly would be her first dinner guest, and definitely her first overnight visitor. She figured there was at least a chance he would fall asleep during dinner.

Elizabeth mulled this over as she waited in the hospital lobby. She'd pulled out the living room sofa bed so he could rest as soon as they got to her apartment, and she had a roast in the crock pot. She felt lucky to have had anything in the freezer. There had been no time to grocery shop.

The lobby elevator dinged and its door opened. Elizabeth thought she kept shock from her expression when the nurse wheeled Skelly out. The phrase *deathly pale* came to mind.

Skelly smiled weakly. "You don't have to look so surprised, Elizabeth."

She shrugged. "I've seen you look better." She glanced at the nurse. "He's good enough to go home?"

"He and the doctor agreed to it, but you're supposed to call if he acts woozy." The nurse took an envelope from the side pocket of her scrubs. "Couple prescriptions, but he has a few pills with him because the pharmacies close early for Christmas Eve. Guidance for you, instructions for him. If you can get him to follow them."

Elizabeth fell into step beside Skelly and the nurse. "I have a whip I can crack."

BUT SHE DIDN'T NEED one. Skelly napped for half-an-hour on the sofa bed, and looked much better when he awoke about six.

Final Cycle

She brought him a ginger ale and half of a tuna sandwich. "Your color's better. The roast was frozen when I put it in the crock pot, so this'll tide you over 'til dinner in an hour. If you're hungry."

"You don't have to wait on me, Elizabeth." He took the drink.

She placed the sandwich beside him on the couch and sat in a rocker next to him. "You look better because you're taking it easy. Besides, I'll get you to shovel Edna's sidewalk next time it snows."

He looked around the living room. "I didn't take in much when we got here. You have a cozy place."

She nodded at the two-foot tall Christmas tree on a table in front of the window. "I'm lucky I kept my old tree from college. No time to do anything else."

"You don't have to go back to work?"

"We're done for the day unless someone needs something. Calls will go to county dispatch." She hadn't described the successful search at Blake Wessley's apartment, though she would if he asked for a status update. "I'm covering tomorrow, and we've turned the low-lifes over to the county."

They lapsed into a comfortable silence. Skelly broke it. "Hard to believe the past week started with a shove in a laundromat." He sipped his ginger ale. "Some people would say she brought it on herself, but from what you told me about that scrapbook, she was a woman in great pain."

"Yes, but why create so much for others?"

"So no one would get close to her, and she would never hurt as much as she did when her younger sister died."

Elizabeth stared at Skelly for several seconds. "That's pretty darn profound."

"In a couple of weeks, or whenever seems like a good time, I'm going to ask Jerry Pew if I can write an editorial about people in pain and how to more constructively address it."

"You see a lot of them."

"Too often when their pain has killed them by drinking, fighting, whatever. They either don't know how to ask for help, or they're so difficult to deal with that no one wants to take time to find out why they act the way they do."

"In my experience, asking criminals why they did what they did doesn't often get a useful answer."

"Wrong question," Skelly said.

"What's the right one?"

"Believe it or not, Oprah Winfrey just came up with it."

"How many pain pills did you take?"

"I'm serious. I saw her interviewed on *Ellen*."

"You're at work when *Ellen* comes on."

"Yes, but some of my work is so awful I keep the TV on for diversion. Anyway, Oprah says when someone acts out, instead of asking 'Why did you do that,' we should ask, 'What happened to you?' In other words, you're asking them why they hurt. It gets at the root of the issue."

Elizabeth looked beyond Skelly to the cornflower blue curtains that framed the living room window. "By the time folks get to me..." she shrugged, "isn't that more for a social worker or therapist?"

"Ideally, and when a kid is young. But somebody has to ask it. There are times when the police could."

Elizabeth didn't want to argue with him. "I suppose, sometimes."

Skelly pointed his sandwich at her. "That college kid, Monty. From the Halloween party last fall."

She nodded. "Someone like him, I guess. He's been in alcohol treatment, and he's home for a break. Came to the station a couple days ago."

They didn't speak for half a minute. Skelly leaned into the back of the couch and shut his eyes. Elizabeth wondered if he was about to doze off with the remains of his sandwich in his lap.

He opened his eyes. "So, what happened to you?"

"Excuse me?"

He grew serious. "You always keep me at a distance."

"How hard was that bump on your head?"

"See, you're doing it now." When she didn't say anything, Skelly said, "You don't have to answer me. But I figure something in your past wants you to keep me out of your future."

Elizabeth stared at him. "Blunt, aren't we?"

He grinned. "Probably was a pretty hard swat to the skull."

She drew a breath. "In Chicago I got involved with another officer. Lots of rules about no fraternization."

Skelly shrugged. "Kind of old-fashioned."

"People date other people in a big department, but...not usually their boss."

"Ah. I know you didn't get fired, though."

"Not even asked to resign. We both got our hands slapped, I got reassigned."

"And you broke up?" Skelly asked.

"Kind of got worn out by the attention. But I could tell, let's see, how to put this? I could tell that it wasn't going to affect his career at all."

"But yours would be?"

"Some people saw it as sleeping with the boss to get ahead. Ironically, especially the other women officers."

"So you decided to leave?"

"I'd had a couple grisly crime scenes with kids. I kind of liked the idea of getting out of Chicago."

"And you like it in Logland." Skelly said it as a statement, not a question.

"Pretty much. But I decided I'd be smarter." She smiled. "Obviously half the guys on my force could be my father, or at least my uncle. I'm not going to date anyone I work with. Ever."

"But, Elizabeth, we don't work together."

"Yesss, but..." She shrugged.

"I mean, I could get you in good with a couple of corpses, but that's the only advantage I can think of."

"I could put poison in your meat, you know."

"Yeah, but whoever did the autopsy would figure it was you."

She sighed and leaned her head against the rocker. "This is complicated."

"Life is complex, but you might be the one who's making it complicated."

Elizabeth studied him. "This conversation is giving you good color in your cheeks." She smiled.

"I'm talking about a date sometime, Elizabeth, not putting a marriage announcement in Jerry Pew's paper."

Without warning, the cat jumped on the sofa bed, walked directly to Skelly, and sat on his chest.

He scratched her head and grinned. "Your cat likes me." He took a piece of tuna from the sandwich and held it out to the cat.

"She likes anyone who feeds her."

He shook his head slightly. "Think about it. I could be dying here. My last chance for a good time."

She raised her eyebrows.

He rolled his eyes, then winced. "Not like 'for a good time call Elizabeth.' After I'm back on my feet, we go to a movie. We can go to a theater fifty miles away if you want."

"Can you cook anything besides Reubens and hamburgers?"

He grinned. "Scrambled eggs, no salads."

"I'll think about it."

Skelly looked at the cat. "I told you her name should be Lucky. You think I'll get lucky?"

Elizabeth stood. "In your dreams."

"I'm on drugs. I've had some pretty weird ones the last day or so."

Elizabeth bent over and kissed Skelly's cheek. "Be nice to Lucky while I finish Christmas dinner."

*   *   *

Thank you for reading Final Cycle. Authors love reviews. If you enjoyed the book, please consider leaving a review at the site at which you purchased the book.

Final Cycle
NICK'S DINER CHILE *

1 Tablespoon oil
1 pound ground beef or turkey
1 onion, chopped
1 green pepper, chopped
2-3 cloves of garlic, minced
1 teaspoon salt
1/2 teaspoon pepper
1 Tablespoon chili powder
1 teaspoon coriander
1 teaspoon oregano
1 can (14 oz) diced tomatoes
1 can each black beans and red beans, drained
2-3 cups tomato juice
Water or chicken stock, as needed

> * Nick's dish is really the chile recipe of
> talented cook Jodi Perko.

Heat the oil in a large pot and add meat, breaking it into small pieces with the back of a fork, and stirring it occasionally until the meat is thoroughly browned. Remove the meat and set aside, leaving the remaining oil in the pan.

With the heat on medium-high, add the onion and pepper, stirring occasionally until the vegetables begin to soften. Stir in the garlic, salt, pepper and spices, (including cayenne, if using) continuing to cook until vegetables are soft and spices are fragrant. Return the meat to the pan, combining it with the vegetables and spices.

Add the tomatoes with the juices, the drained beans, and tomato juice. Stir all together, and add water or stock, 1 cup at a time, if the chili is too thick. Bring to a simmer and taste to adjust for seasoning. Feel free to add more salt, chili powder, etc.

Turn heat down to low. Now is the time to add additional ingredients (such as corn, cooked brown rice.). Cover pot and simmer for 20-30 minutes, stirring occasionally.

Serve hot, offering a variety of mix-ins: shredded cheese, chopped green onions, oyster crackers, chopped avocado, bottled hot sauce, etc.

Books by Elaine L. Orr

If you don't find a book in your local bookstore ask them to order a copy or check the library. All books are in paperback, ebook, and often audio formats.

The Logland Series
Police procedurals with a cozy feel in small town Illinois
Tip a Hat to Murder
Final Cycle
Final Operation

The Jolie Gentil Cozy Mystery Series
The Jersey Shore can be fun with friends–except for the murders.
Appraisal for Murder
Rekindling Motives
When the Carny Comes to Town
Any Por t in a Storm
Trouble on the Doorstep
Behind the Walls
Vague Images
Ground to a Halt
Vague Images
Holidays in Ocean Alley
The Unexpected Resolution
The Twain Does Meet (novella)
Underground in Ocean Alley
Aunt Madge and the Civil Election (long short story)
Sticky Fingered Books
New Lease on Death

The Rivers Edge Series
Iowa nice meets murder along the Des Moines River.

The Family History Mystery Series
Truths of old to solve crimes today in the Maryland Mountains.

About Elaine L. Orr

Elaine L. Orr writes four mystery series: the Jolie Gentil series at the Jersey shore, the River's Edge series along Iowa's Des Moines River, the Logland series in small-town Illinois, and the Family History Mystery series in the Western Maryland Mountains.

What makes Elaine's fiction different from other traditional mysteries is the dry humor and the empathy her characters show to others. Fiction can't 'lecture' readers. But it can contain people whose paths we cross every day — whether we know it or not.

Elaine also writes plays and novellas, including her favorite, *Falling Into Place*. *Behind the Walls* was a 2014 Chanticleer Mystery and Mayhem Award shortlister, and *Demise of a Devious Neighbor* was shortlisted in 2017. *The Unscheduled Murder Trip* received an Indie BRAG Medallion in 2021. Elaine is a member of Sisters in Crime and the International Book Publishers Association.

http://www.elaineorr.com
http://www.elaineorr.blogspot.com
https://www.instagram.com/elaine.orr1/

Printed in the USA
CPSIA information can be obtained
at www.ICGtesting.com
LVHW021345051023
760085LV00064B/1893